SKATING ROUND THE POPPY

Skating Round the Poppy

M.S. Power

MAINSTREAM
PUBLISHING

EDINBURGH AND LONDON

First published in Great Britain 1992 by
MAINSTREAM PUBLISHING COMPANY (EDINBURGH) LTD
7 Albany Street
Edinburgh EH1 3UG

ISBN 1 85158 467 6 (cloth)

Subsidised by the Scottish▲rts Council

A catalogue record for this book is available from the British Library.

Typeset in Plantin by CentraCet, Cambridge
Printed in Great Britain by
Mackays of Chatham Plc

*This book is dedicated with affection and gratitude
to Joseph McLeod of Dundee,
without whose help and guidance it
probably would never have been written*

'We die with love and never dream we're dead.'

Holmes, *Prologue, ad finem*

BOOK ONE

DUNDEE

I

He sits, and stares, and listens. His hands are stuck deep in the pockets of his green-grey anorak, his body stiff and tense. He is alone in the room and is almost glad of the respite although the aloneness still makes him nervous.

It is a small room with a formica-topped table and three chairs on one of which he perches. All the chairs are identical, plastic and metal-framed, the sort that can easily be stacked one upon the other. Mum had some in the garage: 'reserve' chairs she called them, and trotted them out a few times each year for the charity functions she was involved in. The table has burns on the edges. Regularly spaced, they look like crude inlay. Across the room, fixed to the wall on metal brackets, is a black tape-recorder. Even now, switched off, it is oddly menacing.

The walls of the room are dull, avocado green, lumpy and bulging where the plaster has been botched: Irish plastering, Dad would have said. There is linoleum on the floor, mutely patterned grey, and worn, and the ceiling is white with grey patches. There is a jagged crack in the plaster of the ceiling, running from one corner to the other, and curving in and out like the coastline of some exotic South American country, Chile perhaps. He narrows his eyes and follows the crack, weaving his head to trace the contours, but this makes him feel dizzy so he widens his eyes again, stretching them, grimacing with a sort of yawn. There are two narrow windows set high in the wall behind him. They have thick glass with wire mesh embedded in it. To his left is the door, and this door has a square panel of the same glass: through it he can just make out the shapes of people gathered in the corridor outside, huddled, talking. Talking about him probably, trying to decide some new tactic that will make him reveal his name. He hasn't told them that yet. Indeed, he has told them nothing, just sitting there and staring at them with red-rimmed eyes, large grey eyes filled with quiet resignation and sorrow, but mostly sorrow.

He leans back in the chair and the plastic screeches against the metal where one of the screws has been loosened. He rocks gently, turning the piercing noise into the semblance of a tune, a grating lament, something like the metallic twang a badly tuned electric guitar might produce, he thinks, played by some guitarist hoping to make the big time. He gives a small smile, and stops the noise. He sticks one foot out and stares at it, wishing his clothes had been cleaner when they caught him, and that he had shaved. Being unkempt puts him at a disadvantage, like being caught naked. His jeans are stained and frayed at the cuffs. His T-shirt (white, bearing a scurrilous portrait of the Pope with a joint in one hand, and the blasphemous proclamation, I LIKE THE POPE, THE POPE SMOKES DOPE) is grubby. His anorak is ripped on one shoulder, a long, uneven tear that leaves the material flapping, and yellowish padding oozing from it like solidifying pus. His trainers are split and leaking, the laces gone. The dark stubble on his face makes him look older by several years, more like twenty-two or three instead of just eighteen. He is tall and thin, and there is an unhealthy grey sheen to his skin, made all the more pallid by the darkness of his curly black hair. His name is Jimmy Crichton.

'Right. Let's hope you're going to be co-operative this time,' the man from the CID says, starting to talk the instant he enters the room and expressing his hope with the hint of a threat as he makes his way to one of the vacant chairs and settles himself on it gingerly as though

4

suspecting it might collapse under his considerable weight. He is a big man, rotund, quite bald, and jolly enough looking. He has a twinkle in his eyes but this, Jimmy has learned, can change in a flash to a spark of anger. For such a big man he has remarkably small, pudgy hands, and they sweat a great deal. He rubs them together a lot, almost as if constantly washing them. Now he waits for his colleague, a taller, thinner man with a clipped moustache, to organise himself. 'Ready?' he asks, a bit testily.

'Almost, sir.'

'Get a move on.'

The thin man opens two fresh tapes, and inserts them into the recorder. He brings a small microphone on a stand to the table and talks into it, giving the time, saying this is an interview with the suspect and that those in attendance are Inspector William Carter and Sergeant Peter Hayes. He gives the date too: December 20th. Then he sits down and leans back in his chair, waiting for the inspector to take over.

The inspector folds his chubby hands, cocking his head as though still expecting some reply to the statement he made when he first came into the room. In the silence that follows he sighs like a truly saddened man. 'We'll find out who you are eventually, you know. It would be much easier if you just told us. Easier for you, I mean.' He pauses, and stares unblinkingly at Jimmy, his eyes still melancholy. 'You're in deep trouble, young man,' he adds quietly. 'Up to your neck in it,' he concludes, ominously drawing a finger across his neck as though cutting his throat terminally.

Jimmy gives a thin, tired smile.

Instantly the inspector's melancholy vanishes. His eyes are cold and hard when he snaps, 'This isn't any laughing matter, you little toe-rag. There's a dead man out there, and we all know you're the one who topped him.'

Jimmy wipes the smile from his lips.

As if by magic the sadness returns. There is even a hint of a twinkle, and the inspector leans forward, spreading his hands in a curious gesture of supplication. 'Look, all we want to know is who you are, and what exactly happened. We just want to help you.'

Jimmy wants to smile at that too, but he doesn't dare. He looks away. Somehow a wasp has found its way into the sealed room. It

5

seems very drowsy, or maybe injured. It doesn't fly, but tries to crawl up the wall, falling back each time, yet trying again and again until it finally loses the energy to try any more. It curls itself up, lying quite still on the floor, letting its wings hang. Jimmy closes his eyes. 'Jimmy,' he says quietly. 'Jimmy Crichton.'

The inspector pounces on that. 'That's your name? Jimmy Crichton?' he asks, leaning forward, and Sergeant Peter Hayes leans forward too as if that is expected of him.

Jimmy nods.

The inspector lets breath escape slowly from his lungs, making a hissing noise through his teeth, and the sergeant, perhaps mistrusting machinery, decides to write the name down in a notebook. He writes it carefully, spelling the surname aloud.

'My mum always calls me James,' Jimmy volunteers.

The inspector nods with his shoulders. 'Mums don't like abbreviations, do they?'

'Mine doesn't.'

'No,' the inspector says as if he understands something secret. 'I've a brother called Paddy, but *my* mum always insisted on calling him Patrick. She said Paddy sounded too much like a brand of whisky,' he confides with a small grin. 'Where do you come from, Jimmy?'

'Dundee.'

'Dundee, eh? You've come a long way.'

'Oh, yeah. A long way.'

II

Broughty Ferry was once a small, attractive fishing village, but as the city of Dundee grew, it surrounded and overshadowed the village, threatening to swallow it. But for all that, Broughty Ferry managed to retain a certain exclusivity. It was where nice people lived, not brash, moneyed folk like the jute and jam barons who needed to do conspicuous, silly things like erect monuments to themselves in order to prove their fleeting importance, but respectable people, the ones you could look up to: bankers, solicitors, doctors.

Dr Cameron Crichton inherited his father's house in Broughty Ferry. He inherited his medical practice also, and most of his father's patients. It was a fine house, solid and imposing, screened from the road by a high, clipped hedge, and surrounded by a garden that was meticulously kept free of weeds. The doctor's wife, Alice, saw to that. She was a dull, unimaginative woman who treated weeds in the way she treated anything unpleasant that dared encroach on her ordered life: she had them removed instantly, and instantly forgot about them. She was a plain woman, too tall for her liking, and prudish. Everything was categorised in her mind, and labelled. Sex was 'dirty', and she still shuddered to herself when she thought of what she had gone through to produce her only child. She was the sort of woman whose first reaction on seeing a pretty child was to give a motherly sigh, but then her mind would slip back to the moment of conception, and her lips would pucker, and she would recoil slightly from the child as if it were tainted. But she was proud of her husband, and fastidious in her efforts to live up to the standards she believed a doctor's wife should maintain, always appearing nicely groomed, and keeping her voice low and sympathetic. She was proud of her son also, although she worried from time to time that James tended to be withdrawn, even surly, not always bothering to answer when she spoke to him. 'It's as though he didn't even hear me,' she confided to her husband.

'He's at that age,' Cameron Crichton told her, and she accepted that as sound medical diagnosis although, like most things her husband said, she wasn't quite sure what it meant. 'He'll grow out of it,' the doctor assured her, perhaps spotting her puzzlement.

'His last school report wasn't at all good,' Alice persisted. 'He used to get such *good* reports. I do hope he's not mixing with the wrong element.'

Dr Crichton frowned as though, trying, despite the odds, to concentrate on his newspaper.

'The High School isn't like it used to be, you know,' Alice said with a sigh. 'They seem to be letting every sort of ruffian in there now. Not at all the way it used to be.'

'Nothing is,' her husband replied, and shook his newspaper to terminate the conversation.

'Funny name that,' the CID sergeant points out like he wanted to be friendly. He repeats the name. 'Broughty Ferry.' He smiles to himself. He had written down 'Brouty Ferry' but had seen that wasn't right, certainly didn't look right, and changed it.

'Yeah,' Jimmy agrees.

'Sounds nice though.'

'It's all right.'

'Why did you leave home, Jimmy?' the inspector interjects suddenly.

Consciously Jimmy doesn't flinch, but smiles quietly to himself. So that was the way they were going to operate: try and catch him on the hop. After a moment he shrugs extravagantly.

'There must have *been* a reason,' the inspector insists. He leans back in his chair and clasps his hands behind his head. 'Let's see,' he says, mostly to himself. 'In 1988 you said, didn't you? So you were sixteen when you left. A bit young to be setting out on your own, wasn't it?'

Jimmy shrugs again.

'Did something happen to make—?'

'No.'

'You didn't get up to any mischief?'

'No.'

'Didn't have us—the police—calling at the house?'

'No.'

'No row with your parents either, I suppose?'

'No.'

'Just packed your bag and left?'

'That's right.'

'Just like that?'

'Yes.'

'No reason at all?'

'No.'

'Just woke up one morning and said bugger this I'm off?'

'Something like that.'

'Nothing like that. You're a lousy liar, Jimmy Crichton,' the inspector tells him, but kindly.

Jimmy stares at the motionless wasp. After a couple of moments it seems to give a few small kicks with its tiny legs as though terrified by the prospect of approaching death and determined to fight it. Then it lies still again.

Suddenly the inspector makes up his mind about something. 'Well, it doesn't really matter to us why you left home. If you don't want to tell us, that's okay.' He leans forward and places his elbows on the table. His voice takes on a monotonous tone. 'Right. You'll be charged now, and then there'll be other people wanting to talk to you.'

'What people?'

'Just people who want to help,' the inspector said, but he sounded dubious and a bit jaded.

9

'I don't need help.'

The inspector grinned. 'You mightn't think so, Jimmy, but you sure as hell do. Anyway, it's part of the system. Nothing to worry about. They'll be on your side.'

'I bet.'

'Think I'm lying?'

Jimmy gives a small snort.

The inspector doesn't like that. '*I* happen to think it's all a load of crap—all these psychological and social worker reports. If I had my way I'd have you charged, convicted and throw away the bloody key.'

'Yeah, I bet you would. But you can't do that, can you?'

'Don't push your luck, sunshine.'

'You have to make a report. A *full* report. That's the new thing, isn't it? Just so you can't stitch me up.'

'Oh. I see. So that's what you think, is it, smart arse? Well, that's where you're wrong. We know you did it, you were caught standing over the bloke with the knife in your hand, and you've admitted it, so all I have to do is see you get to court safely and in one piece—more or less.' The inspector pauses. 'Don't even have to know the motive—that's old silent movie stuff. Mind you, I'd *like* to know.'

Jimmy looks away.

'Tell me something,' the inspector says, lowering his voice confidentially.

'The reason you killed him—anything to do with why you left home?'

'Shit, no.'

The inspector stays silent.

'No, I said,' Jimmy insists.

The inspector stays quiet.

Jimmy starts to fidget. 'Anything else?' he demands.

'You're sure?'

'Sure about what?'

'That the killing had nothing to do with your leaving home?'

'Yeah, I'm sure.'

'If you say so.'

'I say so.'

But the pert young lady who talks to him an hour later seems convinced that the motive *has* something to do with why he left home. She says so, putting her elbows on the table and leaning forward to make their little chat intimate.

'People do things for all sorts of reasons, James,' she begins, and looks quite taken aback and hurt when Jimmy corrects her. 'I'm sorry,' she apologises and starts again. 'People do things for all sorts of reasons, *Jimmy*,' she says. 'And some of those reasons stem from something—some trauma—you know what that means?—good—some trauma that happened years earlier. Even something completely forgotten by the *conscious* mind. That's why it's so important that we learn as much as possible about your background.' She smiles nicely. 'We're not just prying for the fun of it, you know. Even Inspector Carter—the man you spoke to earlier—the man you gave your name to—even he can't believe that you're just some mindless young thug who killed for the sake of killing. There *are* individuals who act like that—mindlessly—but we don't think you're one of them.'

'Maybe I am.'

The woman smiles nicely again, and takes her elbows off the table. 'No, you're not, and you know it as well as we do.'

'You police too?'

'Good heavens, no!'

Jimmy fixes his eyes on her face and waits. It's a pretty enough face. And the eyes are pretty too. Dark brown. Like Mum's. Maybe even browner. And wider apart. It's not a pinched face like Mum's.

'I'm what they call a child psychologist,' the woman explains, and blushes a little.

Jimmy smiles. 'One of those, eh?'

'Yes, Jimmy. One of those, I'm afraid.'

'Pass me one of those, would you, dear?' Mum said.

'One of what?'

'A wooden spoon, dear. A wooden spoon.'

It was the day before his fifteenth birthday, and Mum was making his birthday cake like she did every year, and every year she said the same thing, 'Soon won't be enough room for all the candles.'

'Mum?'

'Yes, James?'

'Can I talk to you a sec?'

'Of course you can, dear—but don't say "sec". It's vulgar,' Mum said, turning a page. 'What is it?' she asked, still not looking up, sucking one finger as she read down the recipe. '*Two* eggs,' she said to herself. 'Beat in *two* eggs,' she said aloud, and then, 'What is it, dear?' she asked again as if she'd forgotten she'd asked it already.

Jimmy sighed. 'Nothing.'

Mum glanced up at him for a moment. 'I *do* wish you wouldn't do that, James. It's most irritating.'

'Do what?'

'Say you want to talk to me, and when I ask you what you want, you say nothing. You keep doing that, you know.'

'No I don't.'

'Yes you do, dear.' Mum was adamant.

'If I do it's because I know you're not listening.'

'Of course I'm listening. Really, James.' She turned from the table and went to the fridge. She had the egg carton in her hands when she said, 'Now. I'm listening. What was it you wanted to talk about?'

'Would you ask Dad to stop—to stop trying to mess with me?'

Mum gave a little chuckle, and deftly cracked an egg on the side of the mixing bowl. 'What ever do you mean, dear?' she asked lightly, cracking the second egg, and starting the electric mixer.

'You're not listening.'

'Pardon, James?' She switched off the mixer.

'You're not listening.'

'I *am*, dear, but I do have to get this finished or it will never be ready. It takes hours to bake. You can't rush fruit cakes, you know.' She frowned suddenly. 'And what do you mean—messing? Giving out to you? He doesn't do that very often, now does he?' She started the mixer again.

'Turn that off!' Jimmy shouted.

Alice Crichton jumped, and switched off the machine. 'Really, James, there's no need to shout at me.'

'I want you to tell him to stop trying to fuck me.'

In the silence that followed Mum gave a little simper. It was her odd small way of dealing with everything she didn't quite fathom, perhaps giving herself time to digest what had been said, or maybe it was her way of telling people that whatever they had said wasn't all that significant, or that it wasn't worth making a fuss about since things had a way of working themselves out, usually for the best, if ignored. But now she choked on her simper. She pushed the mixer to one side, and stood stock still staring at the bowl for a while. Then she reached, groping, for the wooden spoon, and started stabbing the mixture. Without looking up she asked very slowly, 'What did you say, James?'

'You heard me.'

'Repeat it, please,' Mum said coldly.

'You heard me.'

'I said—repeat it.'

'You heard me.'

Suddenly Mum was across the kitchen and in front of him, hitting him across the face and head as hard as she could with small, clenched fists, screaming, 'You filthy, disgusting child—'

'Mum—'

'—how dare you say something like that about your father! How dare you. Get out of my sight this instant, you filthy, filthy child!'

'Mum, I—'

'Get up to your room this moment. Out of my sight. Just you wait until your father gets home and hears about this!'

'Mum, it's true! I swear it is. He's been trying for—'

Mum put her hands over her ears and stepped back, shaking her head and closing her eyes. 'I don't want to hear another word,' she screamed. 'Not one more word of this awful dirt!' She backed away from him, retreating to the far side of the kitchen table. 'Do what I said,' she shouted. 'Go to your room. Out of my sight this instant!'

Lying on his bed Jimmy heard the mixing bowl smash on the tiled floor of the kitchen. He heard his mother furiously trying to sweep it up. Broken pottery was thrown into the rubbish bin outside the back door, and the metal lid slammed back on. Then there was a strange quiet, and in that quiet he heard his mother sobbing, great heaving sobs. He raised himself on one elbow. He desperately wanted to run downstairs again and comfort her. He even wanted to lie and tell her he'd made it all up if it would stop her crying. He swung his feet off the bed. The kitchen door was thrown open. It swung back, hitting the wall with a thump. Mum, still crying, came up the stairs. She was talking to herself. 'Filthy, filthy, filthy,' she repeated over and over. She went into her bedroom and closed the door, locking it. Jimmy decided to leave her alone. He lay back on his bed and closed his eyes. Although he tried not to, he could not stop himself shaking.

Miss Pimm, the child psychologist, says reassuringly, 'There's absolutely no need to be scared or embarrassed, Jimmy. If something *did* happen that made you want to leave home, you can tell me. I'm sure I won't be shocked or think any the less of you. You'd be surprised at some of the things I've heard.'

'Nothing happened.'

Miss Pimm waits with an understanding smile, a smile clearly well practised and rehearsed, a persuasive smile that usually works.

'I just kept causing them to row,' Jimmy tells her. 'That's all.'

'How was that?'

'How was what?'

Miss Pimm changes her understanding smile to one of tolerance. 'How did you keep causing your parents to row?'

Jimmy grimaces. 'You know. Doing things I shouldn't.'

'What sort of things?'

'Just things. Acting the fool.'

'Most boys act the fool. It doesn't make their parents have rows,' Miss Pimm points out in a tone that indicates experience in such matters. 'Not rows that make the child feel he has to leave home anyway,' she adds with a small raising of her eyebrows.

'This was different.'

'Oh? In what way different?'

'Just different. Look, I don't want to talk about it—okay?'

Jimmy is surprised and relieved when Miss Pimm answers, 'All right, Jimmy. We don't have to talk about anything you don't want to talk about. I'm not here to bully you into saying anything you don't want to. Nobody is. That would be quite pointless.' She glances at her watch, and feigns astonishment. 'Dear me, is that the time already!'

'Must be. Time flies when you're enjoying yourself,' Jimmy tells her with a grin.

Miss Pimm finds it amusing also, and gives a tinkling little laugh as she pushes back her chair and stands up. 'I'll tell you what, Jimmy. We'll take a break now and chat some more this afternoon. That will give you a chance to think about what you *do* want to tell me.' She leans forward and looks as if she is about to reach out and touch his hand, but quickly changes her mind when she spots the wary look creep into his eyes. She frowns thoughtfully. 'I'm afraid they'll want to take you back to your cell during the break,' she tells him, but vaguely as if she really wanted to say something different.

'That's all right. You don't have any fags, do you?'

'No. No. I'm sorry. I'm afraid I don't. I could bring you in some this afternoon, though.'

'Thanks.'

'What sort?'

Jimmy gives her a beaming smile. 'Any sort that has tobacco in them.'

Dad enjoyed his pipe. When he got home, no matter what the time, the first thing he did was light his pipe, starting the ritual by tapping it a couple of times in his special ashtray, a lump of hollowed stone that Mum had given him one birthday, saying, 'At least you won't crack *this* one with your dreadful pipe.'

And that evening Jimmy waited to hear the sound. He had stayed in his room all day, waiting. In a curious way he had half expected the noise of the pipe to be comforting, but when it came, the tap, tap, tap sounded absurdly ominous. He curled himself up on his bed and continued to wait in silence.

After what seemed an inordinately long time under the circumstances, Mum left her bedroom and made her way noisily downstairs. This, in itself, was curious since she tended to move silently about the place, making as little noise as possible as if she believed any noise she *did* make would terminally shatter the peace and tranquillity of her home.

Jimmy unwound himself and crept from his room. He sat on the top stair, hugging himself, listening.

'Cameron, I—' Mum began.

'Oh, Alice. Hello,' Dad said. He was busy lighting his pipe for the second time and his voice was muffled.

'Cameron—'

Dad gave one of his dramatic, exaggerated groans as he sunk back into his armchair. 'Another day like today, Alice, and I'll be prescribing a course of Valium for myself.' He gave a generous chuckle. 'Pass me the paper, would you?'

'Cameron—'

'The paper, dear. The paper,' Dad said, sounding a bit surprised since it wasn't like him to have to ask for something twice. 'What's the matter with you? You look as though you've been crying. Not that wretched 'flu again, is it? It's doing the rounds.'

'No, dear. It's just—'

'Just what?' Dad asked, sounding irritated now, wanting to read his paper, consuming the news before supper and leaving the crossword until later.

'Just onions,' Mum told him quietly. 'I had to peel some. That's all.'

Dad gave a short, barking snort. 'I thought you women had solved that problem. Hold them under a running tap as you peel, or something?'

'Cameron, I want to talk to you,' Mum said, and Jimmy tensed.

'Oh, can't it wait, Alice? I really would like to relax for a minute,' Dad replied. But Mum must have made a face since he added immediately, 'All right, dear, what is it? Another damn party or something? Money for charity? What?'

'No, dear.'

Then there was a silence, and Jimmy could imagine his mother getting flustered, probably wringing her hands, looking ashamed and embarrassed, regretting she had ever started the conversation.

'Well?' Dad demanded.

'It's nothing, dear. It can wait until later. It's nothing important.'

Dad sighed. 'Good,' he said. 'I can get on with reading my paper, can I?'

'Yes, dear.'

Jimmy heard Mum leaving the sitting-room, her high heels clicking on the polished wooden floor of the hall that she cared for with the fervour of a nun. He leaned sideways and watched her through the banisters. She *was* wringing her hands. She had almost made the kitchen door when Dad called, 'Where's Jimmy?'

Mum froze. Her hands went to her face in that odd cinematographic gesture of silent celluloid heroines she had adopted as her own. 'Why?' she asked, her voice tight and strained.

'What do you mean—why? I just want to know where the boy is, that's all.'

'Oh.'

'Well?'

'He's—he's in his room.'

'I see. Good. Thank you.'

Mum lost control of herself for a minute. She began to fidget with her hair, and demanded, 'Why did you say that?'

'What?'

'Why did you say that?'

'Say what, for heaven's sake?' Dad sounded baffled.

'Say—good?'

'What on earth is the matter with you this evening, Alice?' Dad's paper rustled as he put it down. 'I just said good because I don't want him out on the streets getting into trouble. That's all. Why else would I say good?'

'I'm sorry, dear. I just—I'm sorry. I'm being silly.'

17

'You certainly are.'

Tell him, Mum, Jimmy wanted to shout, but didn't. He watched Mum go slowly into the kitchen, and then went back to his room.

III

Jimmy Crichton is glad when they take him down to the cell and lock him in. The thick walls and stout, steel-clad door protect him from intruders. For the moment he does not have any sense of being kept in isolation but, rather, that others are being excluded from his privacy, and that pleases him. Even the drunken yodelling of someone further down the block has a comforting ring to it.

He moves slowly about the cell trying to decipher the graffiti scraped into the plaster above the white tiling that goes halfway up the walls: frightened proclamations of undying love by former detainees for lassies called Lynn, or Allison, or Pauline, or Sharon, or Tracey, their anonymous names encased in hearts and lanced by wavy Cupid's arrows. Even had he wanted to add to the forlorn collection Jimmy can think of no name to etch, linking it to his own. Dave, maybe, but he can't very well scrape JIMMY LOVES DAVE. He allows himself a wistful smile at the thought of what reaction *that* would bring, and moves to settle himself on the thin mattress covered with imitation leather, squatting, his legs pulled up under him, his arms clasped about his knees. It has gone very quiet. The drunk has fallen silent, fallen asleep probably. That's what they all said you should do if you got banged up—sleep. That got you out, got you anywhere you wanted to go. Anywhere your dreams took you anyway. Jimmy shudders involuntarily. His stomach rumbles suddenly, and he wonders if anyone is going to feed him. Maybe that's the way they do it—starve you into submission, until you tell them everything they want to know. He closes his eyes and leans back, letting his curled body collapse on to the bedding.

—Are you awake, Jimmy? Dad's voice whispered in his ear, and Jimmy tried to pretend he was asleep but felt himself begin to shake.

—Jimmy? Dad said as he got into the bed and held Jimmy in his arms, his lips nestling against his neck.

—Oh, Jimmy, Jimmy, Dad sighed, holding him close, one hand moving over his body, caressing it, finally settling on Jimmy's penis, playing with it.

—Don't, Dad, Jimmy pleaded.

—Hush, Dad said, and went on playing.

—I don't like it, Dad, Jimmy tried.

But Dad ignored him, starting to breathe heavily, groaning softly, his own penis, long and narrow, moving back and forth between Jimmy's legs. Then he gave a long, low sigh and Jimmy felt the warm, sticky fluid gush out.

'James! James!' his mother's voice called. 'Kindly come down and have your supper.' Her voice was dry and cold.

The meal that evening was grim and silent. Mum took hardly anything, and the little she put on her plate remained uneaten. She pushed the food around with her fork, separating the fish from the potatoes, then mixing them up again, making both into a small pile, then flattening the pile before starting the ritual all over again.

'You're both very quiet this evening,' Dad observed, but in a tone that suggested he wasn't particularly bothered by the silence. 'This is good, Alice,' he commented, munching the fish pie. He liked fish pie. He approved of fish pie—something to do with the oil in the fish being good for the cholesterol.

'More?' Mum asked.

Dad shook his head. 'Enough is enough,' he said philosophically.

'Quite,' Mum let slip, and stood up quickly to take away the dirty plates and put them on the sideboard. 'I didn't have time to make a pudding,' she said curtly, sitting down again. She always said pudding, never sweet or dessert—pretentious nonsense was how she described those two words. Pure affectation, she sometimes added.

'No pudding?' Dad asked in mock alarm. He liked his puddings too. Nothing fancy, just good home-made puddings like spotted dick, and bread and butter pudding, and treacle tart.

'No. I simply didn't have time.'

'Mum made my birthday cake,' Jimmy said, trying to rescue her.

'There's cheese if you want it,' Mum said, ignoring Jimmy. 'Stilton and some Brie.'

Dad gave a little laugh, and looked over his spectacles at Jimmy. For some odd reason he always wore his spectacles when eating although he really only needed them for reading. 'Was that a hint?' he asked in a good-humoured way. 'Don't worry. I hadn't forgotten. Ordered your present today. You'll like it.'

And Jimmy knew he would like it. Dad was great at that, pleasing people. He always said the right thing, and did the right thing. And he always *looked* right. That was what people always said. His clothes were perfect for a doctor, always understated and solid and comfortable and expensively cut. His face, too, suited his medical calling. When serious, listening to some woe, it adopted a curious tranquillity, the long lines that ran down his cheeks giving him a paternal air. And when he had good news for some patient, and smiled, those lines vanished, and his face became youthful and joyous. And it was this face he presented to Jimmy at the supper table.

'Do you *want* cheese?' Mum snapped.

Dad dismissed Mum's offer with a casual wave of his hand. 'Aren't you going to ask what it is?' he asked Jimmy. 'You do every year.' That was another thing about Dad: regularity. He hated change. Everything had to go like clockwork, and any intrusion into his routine made him irritable. He argued a lot with Mum about the dinner parties she arranged for them to attend, and sometimes he even refused to go, making her go alone since she was so damn keen. And he was meticulous about his property. What was his was definitely his, and he disliked anyone meddling with it. There was a place for everything and woe betide anyone who shifted things. This extended even to the garden tools, all stainless steel and hung on hooks as clean and neat as surgical instruments. He never gardened himself, but he would inspect his tools, and would be grumpy for hours if he found dirt on any of them.

Jimmy asked, 'What is it?'

Mum asked, 'Do you want coffee?'

Dad asked, 'Aren't you going to guess?'

Mum said, 'I asked if you wanted coffee?'

Dad said, 'Yes, but not instant.'

Jimmy said, 'A Ferrari.'

Dad laughed.

Mum scowled.

Jimmy flicked his eyes from his father to his mother, and then fixed them on the pretty arrangement of roses in the centre of the table.

'Not a Ferrari, I'm afraid,' Dad admitted, still laughing. 'Not this year anyway. Probably never at the rate your mother gets through money,' he added and gave Jimmy a conspiratorial wink.

Mum was on the point of standing up, but she sank slowly back into her chair, a bit like a snake recoiling, looking furious. 'And what's that supposed to mean?' she demanded coldly.

'What, dear?'

'That remark about the way I get through money.'

'Just a joke, Alice. A joke. J-O-K-E—joke,' Dad told her with a bit of an exasperated sigh and this time raised his eyebrows at Jimmy.

'Well, in very poor taste then,' Mum snapped.

It was as if only then, at that precise moment, that it dawned on Dad that something was amiss. He looked about him as if trying to locate the tension that surrounded the table. The smile left his face, and he scowled the way he did when about to give a patient bad news, pursing his lips. 'What is the *matter* with you this evening, Alice?'

Mum bridled. 'There's nothing the matter with *me*,' she said. '*I'm* perfectly all right, thank you very much.'

Dad sighed and put his elbows on the table. 'Okay—tell me what I've done—or what I haven't done,' he said resignedly.

Jimmy froze.

For several seconds Mum stared unblinkingly at Dad, purposefully avoiding looking at Jimmy. Her tongue darted in and out of her mouth like an adder's, wetting her lips, making her lipstick shine. She raised one hand and smoothed her hair back over one ear. Then, abruptly, she stood up. 'I'll get the coffee,' she said.

'Women!' Dad said under his breath. 'We'll never understand them, will we, son?'

Mum continued to walk to the door, but stiffly now as if her limbs had mysteriously become wooden. 'Perhaps I'm in the way?' she asked without turning round, and keeping her voice low and even.

Dad made a puzzled grimace but said nothing, leaving Mum standing there, knowing she would be feeling foolish without a reply to latch on to.

The keys jangle and the cell door opens. 'Here we go, young fella,' a constable in uniform, says cheerfully. 'Get that inside you before your belly thinks your throat's been cut.' He hands Jimmy a small plastic tray.

'Thanks,' Jimmy says, staring at the brown mess on the tray. The constable grins. 'It tastes better than it looks,' he says.

'It'd need to. What is it?'

'A Patel special. Curry. A chicken curry, they said.'

'Oh.'

'Could be cat.'

'Probably is.'

'You're lucky, you know. It was Cornish pasties yesterday and you have to sign a special form before you eat those—just so you can't sue us.' He laughs hugely, his whole body shaking with mirth, and Jimmy gives him a small smile to encourage him. 'About as Cornish as I am,' the constable adds but letting his laughter drift away and his face become serious as he asks, 'You all right, son?'

'Yeah. I'm fine.'

The constable nods. 'Good. Good. Nothing's ever as bad as it seems, you know.'

'So they say.'

'And it's true.'

'If you say so.'

'I do indeed. Seen most things in my life and there's always a simple way round most problems.'

'That's great.'

'You'll not be thinking of doing anything stupid, will you?'

'Hell, no.'

The constable nods again approvingly. 'Good.'

'Good, eh?' Dad asked, standing back to admire his handiwork.

'Smashing,' Jimmy said.

'You really like it?' Dad sounded anxious.

'It's great. Just what I wanted. Thanks, Dad.'

And the computer was indeed a great affair, and it had all the gadgetry that goes with such things. Dad had even bought a special desk with shelves and drawers, and an executive swivel chair.

'It really *is* what you wanted, isn't it?' Dad asked, putting his arm about Jimmy's shoulder and squeezing.

Jimmy nodded. He felt his muscles go tense. He wanted to move away, away from Dad's arm, yet at the same time he did not want to hurt his father's feelings. 'Dad—?'

'Hmmmm?' Dad was running his finger along Jimmy's neck and round behind his ear.

'Dad, please don't.'

'Shush,' Dad said gently.

'Please, Dad. Don't. I hate it.'

But Dad paid no attention. He only moved closer, putting both

24

arms around him now, holding him close. 'No, you don't hate it, Jimmy,' he said. Jimmy could feel his breath on his neck.

'I do, Dad,' Jimmy said, and pulled himself away. He went across to the bed and sat down. Instantly Dad started to follow. Jimmy stared at him. There was something so sad in his father's eyes, and a curious look of longing that frightened Jimmy. He took a deep breath. 'I told Mum,' he blurted. 'I asked her to tell you to stop.'

At first Dad looked puzzled, then hurt. The blood drained from his face and he started to tremble. Then, suddenly, he was angry, his face flushing. 'You did *what*?' he asked between his teeth.

'I told Mum,' Jimmy said.

Dad looked as if he was about to hit him. His arm rose but flopped back down to his side again. Heavy breath came from his mouth, a sort of panting.

'Dad—'

But Dad was walking from the room, stooped like an old man, his feet shuffling.

'Dad, please—'

Dad closed the door behind him.

The cell door slams and the keys rattle as the lock is turned. The same policeman who brought him the curry has collected his tray and left him a mug of thick, sweet tea, and some advice. 'Just tell them what they want to know, son. It's far easier that way. Nobody's going to think any the worse of you, you know. The sooner you tell them everything, the sooner they'll have the whole thing sorted out.'

Jimmy nods.

'That's better. You're not the first young lad to do something daft. Nor the last.'

Jimmy keeps nodding.

'Anyway, drink your tea and have yourself a bit of a kip,' the policeman tells him. 'And remember—nothing's ever as bad as it seems.'

'I didn't want to, you know,' Jimmy says quietly.

'I don't expect you did, lad. Very few people really *want* to kill another human being.'

'That's not what I meant.'

The constable frowns quizzically. 'What *did* you—?'

'I didn't want to tell Mum,' Jimmy interrupts.

The constable waits in silence.

Jimmy buries his head in his hands.

'Tell your mum what, son?' the constable asks finally, keeping his deep, gruff voice as quiet as Jimmy's.

'About—' Jimmy looks up suddenly, and stares at the ceiling. He shakes his head and gives a tiny smile. 'Nothing,' he says. 'Nothing.'

Jimmy waited before going to the door of his bedroom and opening it a little. He stood there listening, trying to stop himself shaking. He heard Dad make his way down the stairs and go across the hall and into the sitting-room. Then there was nothing for a while. No sound at all. But finally Dad asked, 'What *is* the matter with you, Alice? You've been most odd.' His voice was calm and normal.

Jimmy thought he heard Mum give a little gasp, but he could have imagined it.

'Did you hear me, Alice?'

'Yes,' Mum said.

'Well, would you mind answering me?'

'It's nothing,' Mum said.

'What do you mean—nothing?'

'It's well—it's—' Mum started but stopped, taking a gulp of air. It's—well, it's James.'

'What about him?' Dad demanded.

'He's been saying things.'

'What things?'

'Just things. Silly things.'

—Tell him, Mum. Tell him to leave me alone, Jimmy pleaded to himself.

'Just nonsense,' Mum added.

'Tell me what he's been saying, damn it!' Dad said, shouting.

'That you—oh, it's ridiculous, dear,' Mum sounded frightened.

—Tell him, Mum. Please tell him!

'For God's sake, Alice! Tell me what the boy has been saying. I want to know!'

Mum sounded as if she was in tears when she spoke. 'He asked me to tell you to stop—to stop—to stop messing with him.'

—Thanks, Mum.

'Messing with him?' Dad asked, pretending not to comprehend.

'Yes, dear.'

'What on earth did he mean by that?'

Mum hesitated. 'I don't know, dear.'

'Didn't you ask him?'

'No.'

'Why not?'

'Because I didn't want to know,' Mum said. And then, out of the blue, horribly, she screamed the same words. 'Because I didn't want to know!'

There was a terrible silence, with Mum's scream echoing about the house, and in the silence Dad must have done something, made some face or gesture, that caused Mum to wonder. 'He said you tried to— you didn't, Cameron, did you?' Mum was pleading now.

'Did I what?'

'You didn't try to—'

—Go on, Mum. Please.

'—try to—to abuse him?'

'Is that what he said?'

'Yes.' It was a whisper.

'And you *believed* him?'

'Oh, no, dear. Of course not.'

—Oh, Mum—*please*.

'But—'

'But what?' Dad asked sharply.

'But why would he *say* such a thing, Cameron, if—'

27

'So you *do* believe him!' Dad roared.

'No, dear, I—'

But Dad was no longer listening. 'Well that's just great. Just bloody great. A fine wife you turned out to be.'

'But, Cameron, how—'

'Just shut up, Alice,' Dad hissed. 'I don't want to hear another word from you. I'm going out,' he added, and there was something ominous about the way he said it. He slammed out of the sitting-room, and out of the house, pulling the door behind him with a crash.

For the rest of the evening Alice Crichton remained seated in what she liked to call her 'sewing chair' although she had never been known to sew in her life. Her shoulders were hunched, her arms folded tightly across her breasts as though she was clasping something precious but fleeting to her heart. And she rocked herself from time to time, looking suddenly very old in that frightened grey way that people who have been subjected to lengthy isolation or peremptory loneliness do. It was not until after midnight that she roused herself and went up to bed.

'Mum!' Jimmy called from his room.

'Go to sleep, James,' Mum said tightly, and closed her bedroom door. She'd forgotten to give him his birthday present. Perhaps on purpose. Probably on purpose.

—You shouldn't have told your mother, Jimmy, Dad said. He was drunk and he slurred his words, and fumbled with the blankets as he got into bed beside Jimmy.

—Dad, I—

But Dad wasn't about to listen. He was already groping his way across Jimmy's body, roughly this time, as if there was a particular urgency about his actions now, as if, also, they were some sort of punishment.

Jimmy tried desperately to pull himself from Dad's grasp, but Dad's arms held him tight, pinning him down. You're *mine*, Dad said. Mine.

And then he forced Jimmy on to his stomach and climbed on top of him.

—No, Dad, Jimmy pleaded. Please, he said, but it was just a whisper.

Dad spat on his fingers and wiped the spittle on to Jimmy's rectum. Then he tried to force his penis in. The pain was excruciating, and Jimmy screamed. Immediately Dad clamped one hand over his mouth, and went on pushing. Jimmy bit his father's hand and screamed again.

—Cameron? Mum called from her bedroom. Cameron?

—Shit, Dad swore, and jumped out of the bed, catching his foot in the sheet and toppling on to the floor. Shit, he said again.

—Cameron?

—I'm coming, Dad called.

—What's the matter?

—Nothing. I'm coming.

Alone, Jimmy heard his parents talking, heard Dad say Jimmy had been having a nightmare, heard Mum say how sorry she was about— you know, dear.

—We'll sort it out, Dad told her comfortingly.

—Of course we will, Mum agreed.

Jimmy felt the tears rolling down his cheeks and into his mouth, warm and salty. He bit into the pillow, screaming silently to himself until he fell asleep.

IV

Miss Pimm comes into the room with a bounce, and apologises politely to Jimmy for keeping him waiting. She looks a little bit smug, as if she's found something out during the lunch break, but she's kindly enough, and not crowing. She brings a tall bearded man with her; she brings cigarettes, too, which is the important thing. 'This is a colleague of mine,' she explains to Jimmy. 'His name is Dr Rutherford. You don't mind if he sits in on our talk, do you? Just sits and listens—he won't—I think—' she glances at Dr Rutherford '—interrupt'.

Dr Rutherford shakes his head.

'I don't mind,' Jimmy says.

'Thank you,' Miss Pimm replies. She looks about the room and gives an embarrassed little titter. 'I'm afraid you'll have to go and get yourself a chair, Harry,' she points out.

'Oh. Yes,' says Dr Rutherford, and leaves the room with a strange loping stride like the slow-motion, action-replay of a marathon runner. He has a bald patch on the back of his head, and he has tried to conceal this by combing wisps of hair across it. Unsuccessfully.

Miss Pimm settles herself comfortably in her place. She rummages in her pocket and produces a packet of cigarettes with a small triumphant flurry. 'I didn't forget, you see.' She slides them across the table. 'I hope that brand is all right.'

'Fine. Thanks.'

30

'I only got that sort because I quite liked the packet.'

'You must vote Tory.'

Miss Pimm looked bemused. 'Why do you say that?' she asks, perhaps wondering if the observation is significant.

Jimmy holds up the packet of Regal Kingsize. 'Tory blue,' he points out with a grin.

'Oh,' says Miss Pimm, hesitating a moment before grinning also. 'I see. Well, as a matter of fact, I don't.'

Jimmy shrugs.

'I'm rather more green than blue.'

'Tough,' says Jimmy widening his grin.

Miss Pimm displays a tiny irritation with a series of quick blinks, like someone who is constantly being chided about her curious allegiances, someone who, at the same time, isn't all that convinced of her beliefs. 'Why tough?' she asks.

'Just a wee joke,' Jimmy tells her.

'Oh. Yes. I see.'

'You haven't a match, I suppose?'

Miss Pimm looks blank. 'A match?'

Jimmy has taken a cigarette from the packet, and holds it up. 'A match for this?'

Miss Pimm slaps her hands to her cheeks. 'Oh, Lord. No. I'm afraid I haven't. I never thought. How stupid of me. I'm sorry.' She frowns for a moment. 'I think Harry smokes. Maybe he'll have one. If not I'll go and get you some.'

Dr Rutherford does, indeed, have one. Not a match, but a lighter. He has found a chair and come back into the room, placing the chair against the wall, well away from the table. He offers Jimmy a light, and leaves his lighter on the table with a sympathetic nod. Then he retires to his chair, crossing his long legs, resting one elbow on his knee, and cupping his chin in one hand.

Jimmy sucks the smoke deep into his lungs. At first he feels dizzy. He closes his eyes to stop the room spinning. Soon the dizziness passes, and he takes another deep drag.

'Better?' Miss Pimm asks.

'Much. Thanks.'

'Good.' She opens her folder and spreads some papers in front of her. She folds her hands and looks up. 'Well, now,' she says, and pauses to settle her spectacles more comfortably on the bridge of her nose, giving herself a moment to consider how best to say what she wants to say. She decides to be frank. 'I'm going to be absolutely frank with you, Jimmy, and tell you everything that happens—all right?'

Jimmy nods.

'That way you'll know—I hope—that I'm not trying to trap you into saying anything you don't want to.'

Jimmy nods again. 'Okay.'

'To begin with,' she pauses to take a breath, 'the police have contacted your parents.'

Jimmy feels his body go rigid. Then he feels anger rising inside him. He wants to explode and shout that the police and everyone else should mind their own fucking business, but he spots Dr Rutherford make a small movement and narrow his eyes. 'What'd they want to do that for anyway?' he asks, and leaves it like that.

'They had to be told, Jimmy.'

'No they didn't.'

'I'm afraid they did.'

'They don't care.'

'But they do. You're very mistaken. They care a great deal. They're both very worried.'

'I bet.'

'Especially your father.'

'Oh, well, he would be, of course. A very caring person, my dad is. Very bloody caring.'

Miss Pimm cocks her head. 'He certainly seems to be.'

Jimmy allows himself a sardonic sneer. 'Oh, he is.'

'Anyway, they're coming down to see you.'

'I don't want to see them.'

'I think you should.'

'I don't have to.'

'No. You don't *have* to, of course. But I think you should.'

'No.'

Miss Pimm sighs. 'Well, think about it at least, will you?'

'There's nothing to think about. I won't see them, and that's that.'

Miss Pimm looks perplexed at Jimmy's attitude. She has a pen in her hands and she twirls it round and round in her fingers. It clicks against the ring she wears: a buckle ring in gold on her little finger. She glances at the papers in front of her. She turns her head and gives Dr Rutherford a quick look, and Dr Rutherford gives an imperceptible nod. Miss Pimm clears her throat. 'You're not—not afraid of them, are you, Jimmy?'

Jimmy makes a scoffing snort. 'Of course I'm not afraid of them.'

'You're sure?'

'Sure I'm sure. Why should I be?'

'I just wondered if—never mind. Let's just leave that for the moment, shall we?' she asks tolerantly, but she has that smug little face on again, and Jimmy wonders if she's found out something about his dad.

'Wondered what?' he asks.

'Well, things happen in families.'

'Like what?' Jimmy asks, trying to act innocent.

'Things that are difficult to talk about.'

Jimmy raises his eyebrows.

'Abuse,' Dr Rutherford says clearly, and Miss Pimm gives a small wince.

'Oh, *that*. Incest, you mean. A game for all the family,' Jimmy says, and gives a harsh laugh.

'Like I said,' Miss Pimm interrupts, 'It just seems very odd that you should simply decide to up and run away from what appears to be a comfortable, loving home for no apparent reason.'

'I didn't run away. I just left.'

'Of course.'

'James Crichton! Would you kindly wake up and pay attention,' called Mrs Clarke, the teacher.

'Yes. Sorry, Mrs Clarke.'

'I know it's the last day of term, but that's no excuse to daydream.'

'No, Mrs Clarke.'

'Besides, you did tell me your parents were taking you to France

33

this summer, so I would have thought a little French would have been of particular interest to you.'

'Yes, Mrs Clarke.'

'Ooo-la-la,' scoffed Andy Cox who went abroad every year. 'France with Mummy and Daddy. How *nice*.'

'That'll do, Andrew Cox,' Mrs Clarke snapped, turning sharply back to the blackboard on which she had written, *J'ai besoin d'un—* 'Very important words,' she insisted. '*J'ai besoin d'un*—I have need of—' she intoned.

'Need of what, Mrs Clarke?' Andy Cox wanted to know.

'Of anything you like, Andrew. That's why the words are important.'

'*J'ai besoin d'un* piss,' Andy suggested.

'If you must be vulgar—yes, Andrew. Only do try not to show your ignorance more than you have to. It's pronounced "pee" in French,' corrected Mrs Clarke, taking the wind out of Cox's sails. 'James, would you like to make a slightly more intelligent suggestion?'

'*J'ai besoin d'un ami*,' Jimmy said after a while, instantly wishing he'd thought up something else.

'Excellent, James,' Mrs Clarke said, beaming. 'I like that a lot.' She liked Jimmy a lot too, although she tried hard not to show it since she wasn't one who encouraged favouritism. But she worried about him also: there was something about him that baffled her, something in his eyes, she told herself, something that spoke of terrible loneliness and isolation. And on several occasions he had hung back after class was done, pretending to be tidying up his desk. She sensed he wanted to speak to her, but sensed also that were she to suggest such a thing he would shy away. So, she waited for him to speak, but he never did. 'But you will be careful,' she now advised. 'If it's a lady friend you're referring to, it becomes "*d'une*"—feminine—"*amie*"—with an "e" on the end of both words.'

'No chance *he'll* be going after *une amie*,' Andy Cox interrupted. 'Mummy wouldn't let that happen. Might lose her little precious.'

Mrs Clarke got very annoyed. 'That's quite enough out of you, Andrew Cox,' she said, putting on her steely voice. 'Quite enough. You're getting far too big for your boots, young man.'

'I only—'

'I said enough, Cox. Quite enough.'

'That's quite enough, Cameron,' Mum was saying as Jimmy came into the house through the back door, and stood in the kitchen. 'I really don't want to hear another word about it. You've said there's no truth to what the boy said, and that's all I needed to know.'

'And supposing he's been saying the same thing to other people?'

Mum sounded shocked. 'Oh, I'm sure he hasn't.'

'You can't *know* that.'

'No, I can't *know* it, but he'd never go that far. It's not exactly the sort of thing you go shouting from the rooftops, is it?' Mum said. 'Let's just forget about it.'

'Forget about it!' Dad shouted. 'Not bloody likely. And you can start by cancelling our holiday, that's for sure.'

'There's no need to—' Mum started to protest.

'I said, cancel it.'

'But I've told everyone we're going,' Mum said.

'Well, tell them now you've changed your mind.'

'I can't do that, Cameron.'

'Well, *you* go.'

'And leave you two alone together?' Alice Crichton asked, and immediately realised the enormity of her error. All she had meant was leave you two males alone to cope with the cooking and cleaning but, under the circumstances, it hadn't sounded at all like that. It had come out like an accusation.

'Thank you, Alice,' Dad said in a fierce whisper, forcing the words out through clenched teeth, and for the first time that he could remember Jimmy heard real hatred in his father's voice. 'Thank you very much,' Dad added, and walked heavily from the house, slamming the door behind him. That was the way he seemed to solve every argument now: leaving the house and banging the door.

Mum was sobbing again as Jimmy crept past the sitting-room door

35

and climbed the stairs to his room. He longed to go in to her, to put his arm about her, to say he was sorry for causing all the quarrels but he knew she would dismiss him, waving him away in the way she had when she was in that mood. He went upstairs as silently as a ghost.

When he entered his bedroom he could not believe his eyes at first. Then, slowly, it dawned on him what had happened. His new computer lay on the floor, its screen smashed to smithereens as if someone had put his foot through it in a fit of rage. For a long time Jimmy just stood in the doorway and stared, his mouth open. Then he moved into the room and dropped his schoolbag on the floor. He bent and lifted the shattered computer back on to its desk. He knelt down and methodically began to gather up the shards of glass. He could hardly see them. Tears, hot, angry tears filled his eyes. Finally, he sat back, resting against the bed.

—I'm sorry, Jimmy, Dad was saying, sounding like he was sobbing through his drunkenness. I was just upset. Angry. I'm sorry. I didn't think. I'll get you another computer first thing in the morning. I promise, Dad promised, holding Jimmy tight. Let's make it like it was, he added, pleading.

—You needn't, Dad, Jimmy said, hoping that might make Dad stop feeling him.

But it didn't. And although Dad didn't try to penetrate him again, he did put his penis between his legs and shoved and pushed until he came, sighing all the time: Oh, Jimmy. Oh, Jimmy. Oh, Jimmy.

Only when Mum coughed in her sleep did Dad sneak out of the bed, and stand there naked, listening, making sure it was safe for him to go back to his own room. He didn't say goodnight or anything, just crept out, leaving the door ajar.

Miss Pimm decides to pursue a different tack, and for this she changes her tone, making herself sound very casual as if discussing a recent holiday. 'So,' she says, 'When you left home, where did you go first?'

'Glasgow,' Jimmy tells her.

For some reason this seems to surprise Miss Pimm. 'Glasgow?' she repeats, her voice rising in an arc as though Glasgow were the last place she could imagine anyone going. 'Why Glasgow?'

Jimmy shrugs. 'Dunno. I just went there.'

'Did you know anyone there?'

'No.'

'I see. You could have chosen to go anywhere—it was just a whim that made you choose Glasgow?'

'That's the word for it—a whim,' Jimmy agreed, enjoying that word and letting it hum on his lips. 'Whim,' he repeats. 'That, and the fact that the car was going there,' he adds.

'What car?' Miss Pimm asks sharply, and Dr Rutherford leans forward expectantly.

'The car I got a lift in. I hitch-hiked down, didn't I?'

'Oh,' says Miss Pimm, clearly disappointed, and Dr Rutherford looks a bit forlorn also as he settles back in his chair. 'So if the car had been going to London, say, you'd have gone there instead?'

'Yeah,' says Jimmy. 'If it had been going to Zimbabwe I'd have gone there. Gone anywhere the car was going.'

'I see.'

'I just wanted to get away,' Jimmy volunteers.

Miss Pimm jumps on that. 'Why, Jimmy? Why was it so important to get away?' she asks, and leans forward.

For a moment Jimmy feels like telling her everything. She tries so hard he doesn't want to disappoint her again. He looks away, staring up at the ceiling. Dad's face looms into his consciousness and the sound of his drunken sobbing echoes in his ears. He looks back to Miss Pimm. 'A bit of adventure, I suppose,' he says. 'Everyone wants adventure, don't they?'

'I suppose they do,' Miss Pimm agrees, obviously not believing him but deciding to accept his explanation for the moment. 'And that was the only reason?'

'Yep.'

It was the first day of the summer holidays when he tried to make the peace again. 'Mum—I'm sorry,' he said.

'It's a bit late for sorry now,' Mum replied, not looking at him, and sounding as if she wanted that to be the end of the conversation. She started plumping up the cushions on the settee, whacking them with gusto. But as Jimmy turned to leave, she added, 'I just hope you realise what you've done to us—your father and me.'

'Mum, I—'

'What I *can't* understand is what *we've* ever done to make you tell such—such vicious lies. How could you, James? How could you *say* such things about your own father?'

'Mum, I'm sorry. I didn't want—'

But Mum wasn't listening. 'I could understand it if we'd been unkind to you, or deprived you of anything. But we've given you everything you've ever wanted. Everything. And a lot more than most boys of your age get from their parents, I might add.' She selected another cushion and thumped the feathers into shape. 'What on earth did you hope to gain by making up these dreadful stories?'

'Mum, I didn't—'

'Can't you see the damage it could have done to the whole family if people were stupid enough to believe you?'

'I didn't lie, Mum,' Jimmy said, although he knew it was useless.

Mum hurled the cushion onto the settee and rounded on him. 'Now just you listen to me, young man. If you persist in this catalogue of lies I'll—I'll—I'll—' Mum couldn't think of anything dire enough that she might do, and it was probably her frustration at this that made her shout her favourite phrase, 'Oh, just get out of my sight, and stay out.'

He waited until he was certain that Mum and Dad were asleep: they both had the habit of snoring, and were snoring heavily when he decided to leave.

After supper he had packed the hold-all he used for his sports gear, cramming it with the things he thought he'd need, practical things like underwear, socks, and pullovers ('They're pullovers, dear,' Mum always insisted. 'Only working-class people call them jumpers'). He put on his anorak, a great padded affair that Dad had bought him earlier in the year when Jimmy had been keen on fishing. It made him look twice as fat as he really was, but it was warm and snug and comforting. ('You look like a great cuddly teddy-bear in that, James,' Mum had commented, and Dad had smiled secretly, and Jimmy had blushed.) He emptied his money box. There was more than he thought, nearly seventy pounds including the thirty his grandparents had sent him for his birthday. He put the coins in his jeans pocket and folded the notes, stowing them away in the inside pocket of the anorak. As an afterthought he put his new passport in the pocket with his money. He gazed about the room, taking everything into his memory. Then, quickly and quietly, he went downstairs and left the house, easing the front door shut behind him. When the lock clicked he hesitated, wondering if his parents had heard the sound, in an odd way hoping they *had* heard, and that they would come down and ask him to stay. Nothing happened. The lights in the house stayed out. Everything was silent. He swung his hold-all on to his shoulder and walked to the gate, staying on the grass so that his footsteps wouldn't be heard crunching the gravel. He looked back once as he shut the gate, and then set off down the road.

'Where are you going?' Jimmy asked.

'Glasgow. A bit late for a young lad like you to be out on the road hitch-hiking,' the man said, waiting for Jimmy to put his hold-all on the back seat and get into the car.

'Missed the train,' Jimmy lied, getting in beside the man and strapping on his seatbelt.

'Oh. Well, take my advice and be careful. There's a lot of weirdos about these days, you know, just waiting for nice-looking young lads like you.'

'I'll be all right.'

'That's what we all think. I'll be all right. It always happens to the other fellow. Never to me.'

'Nothing's going to happen to me.'

'I sure hope not. Lucky for you I'm going all the way.'

'Yes.'

'I always travel at night if I can. Less traffic and less hassle. Leaves me time for a kip in the car before I start work. Crazy bloody business—selling. Know what I sell?'

'Tell me.'

'Guess.'

'No idea.'

'You won't believe it.'

'Try me.'

'Knickers!' The man guffawed as if he'd made the funniest joke in the world. 'Well, lady's lingerie they call it now, but it's mostly knickers just the same. Knickers is knickers no matter what fancy French name you put on them, aren't they?'

'I suppose they are,' Jimmy agreed.

The man fell silent for a while. He had a dreamy smile on his face as if he was imagining beautiful women putting on, or taking off, his natty merchandise. The sign for Perth glowed in the headlights before he spoke again. 'And what takes you to Glasgow anyway?'

'Visiting my grandparents,' Jimmy lied, surprised at how glibly the tale rattled out.

'Oh, that's nice.'

'Yeah. They're nice.'

'Grandparents always are. It's parents that are the trouble.' The man laughed again, somewhat bitterly.

'Not always,' Jimmy said. 'My parents are great.'

'Then you're lucky. Want to know what mine did? Dumped me when I was a few months old. In a goddamn park, would you believe. Never did find out who they were. Never bloody wanted to either,' the man told him. 'Wouldn't want to now either. Too late,' he said wistfully. 'Far too late.'

It had started to rain, and the windscreen wipers flicked back and forth monotonously across the windscreen. 'Oh, dear God,' the driver sighed. 'Rain again. Never seems to do anything else but rain, does it? I'll tell you one thing—when I win the pools I'm off to Bermuda to retire in all that lovely sunshine.'

'I hope you win them then,' Jimmy told him, meaning it.

'Can't. Never do the damn things.' The man took to laughing again. Then he asked, 'Whereabouts in Glasgow do you want to be dropped off?'

'Oh, anywhere near the centre. I know it well.'

'Hope Street okay? I can let you out there near the station if that suits you?'

'Fine. Hope Street would be just great.'

'Hey—you want me to stop somewhere on the way so you can call them—your grandparents, I mean?'

'No thanks. I did that in Dundee when I missed the train.'

'Oh, that's okay then. No point in having them worry about you when you're safe and sound.'

'They won't be worried.'

'Not now. Not if you've called them. But they would have been.'

'Yes. They worry a lot.'

'Nice that, though, isn't it? Having someone to worry about you?'

'Oh, terrific.'

Alice Crichton's parents visited Dundee once a year, regular as clockwork. They arrived the first day of June, gaunt, toothless and unsmiling, and left ten days later as dour and forbidding as when they had come. Why they came was something Jimmy had never quite understood. All they did was sit and complain, or sit and sleep. They didn't say much, and ate very little. They slobbered their food and Mum spent much of the time cleaning up after them. Grandad got the shakes a lot, and Gran was pretty deaf, always saying she couldn't hear the television although it was blaring. She liked Jimmy, though, and insisted he sit by her, and she held his hand tight in her bony fingers.

Every year Dad would say, 'This is the last time we're having them.'

'Yes, dear,' Mum would say, but every year they returned since Mum hadn't the heart not to invite them.

Gran told Jimmy once that they didn't really want to leave their bungalow near Kirkcudbright and make the trek to Dundee but they didn't think it would be kind to refuse Mum's invitation. But when Jimmy told Mum, she said, 'You must have misheard, James. They love coming. They look forward to their little visit all year.'

Dad consoled himself with the thought that, 'Well, the only good thing is they can't last that much longer.'

'That's a terrible thing to say, Cameron,' Mum said. 'They're family.'

'Yours. Not mine,' Dad said quickly.

'They're James's grandparents.'

'I'm sure that thrills him.'

'He's very fond of them, and they love him.'

'So, you hitched down to Glasgow,' Miss Pimm says.

'Yep.'

'Was that in the daytime or at night?'

'Night. I had to wait until Mum and Dad were asleep, didn't I?'

Miss Pimm smiles understandingly. 'Yes, I suppose you did. You left them a note?'

Jimmy shakes his head.

'Oh, dear.'

'Hell, I wasn't about to kill myself or anything.'

'No—but—well, it would have been kinder, wouldn't it?'

Jimmy shrugs.

Miss Pimm sighs.

Dr Rutherford blinks.

'Well, you got to Glasgow at night—what did you do with yourself that first night?'

Jimmy stares at her.

'Can't you remember?'

42

'Yeah, I can remember.'

'It can't have been very pleasant for you—all alone in a strange city. Didn't you feel dreadful?'

'I was okay.'

'So, what did you do?'

'Walked about.'

'The whole night?'

'No.'

Miss Pimm waits for more information, and Dr Rutherford uses the silence to uncross his legs.

It was still raining when the knicker salesman let Jimmy out of the car in Hope Street near the station. 'Take care now, pal,' he said cheerfully.

'I will. And thanks a lot.'

'No problem.'

Despite the hour there were still plenty of people wandering about: couples, coming from parties maybe, looking happy, arms entwined; groups of youngsters, bunching together as they walked as though for protection, mostly silent, their eyes flicking about them nervously; a few drunks, staggering along singing to themselves, but some giving up the struggle to stay erect and collapsing in any convenient doorway; and police. Jimmy spotted the police, two of them, coming towards him. Their eyes seemed fixed on him. He decided to brazen it out, walking straight towards them. 'Excuse me,' he said politely.

The police were nonplussed. They stopped in unison, swaying a little on the balls of their feet, eyeing Jimmy with automatic suspicion.

'Could you tell me when the next train leaves for Dundee?' Jimmy asked, keeping the tremor out of his voice.

'What's in the bag?' one of the policemen demanded.

'This? My clothes.'

'Open it.'

Jimmy obligingly opened the bag, and the policeman who had not

43

spoken rummaged in it off-handedly. Satisfied, he nodded to his colleague. 'What's your name?'

'James Crichton.'

'Date of birth?'

'6 July 1974.'

'Address?'

Jimmy told them.

'Dundee, eh? What you up to down here in Glasgow and out on the street at this hour?'

'Trying to catch a train home. I was late leaving my grandparents' house in London so I missed the train I was supposed to get.'

For a moment it looked as though neither of the policemen believed him and were going to make a check. Then two drunks started to brawl on the opposite side of the road, outside the Hard Rock Café, and the policemen stiffened. 'Ask in the station. And keep off the streets.'

They left Jimmy standing there, grinning to himself, and crossed the road in measured, authoritative strides to sort out the drunks.

Miss Pimm cannot bring herself to wait any longer. 'So, what *did* you do with yourself, Jimmy?'

'Sat in an all-nighter and drank coffee.'

'Which all-nighter—do you remember?'

Jimmy nods. 'Dunkin' Donuts, it's called. Lots of kids who have nowhere to go end up there at night.'

'You mean homeless children?'

'Yeah.'

Miss Pimm writes down Dunkin' Donuts carefully. 'You don't remember what street that's on, do you by any chance?'

'Argyle Street—I think. Not sure though. But I think it's Argyle Street,' Jimmy tells her.

Miss Pimm smiles her thanks, and writes down Argyle Street and puts a question mark after it. Then she looks up. 'And that was how you spent your first night away from home—sitting in this Dunkin' Donuts café, drinking coffee?'

'That's how I spent it. Exciting, eh?'

Miss Pimm makes a little face. 'Did you meet anyone there?'

'Not meet. Not the way you mean it. Spoke to people, though.'

'Like who?' Miss Pimm asks, ballpoint poised.

'Just kids. Homeless kids.'

'Do you remember any of their names?'

'We didn't give names. Just spoke.'

'About what?'

'Nothing in particular. Just spoke. Words. There weren't any great philosophical discussions or anything.'

'No. I expect not,' Miss Pimm says tartly. 'And what time did you leave this place?'

Jimmy shrugs. 'Dunno. When everyone else piled out.'

'You went with them?'

'Out of the café, yes.'

'But you didn't stay with them?'

'I went off by myself.'

'Why was that?'

'Because I wanted to be by myself.'

'Weren't you lonely?'

'Not then,' Jimmy tells her. And then, mostly to himself, he repeats, 'Not then.'

'But surely—' Miss Pimm starts to protest, but stops herself when she notes the look in Jimmy's eyes. She knows that look by now. It means Jimmy is no longer listening.

BOOK TWO

GLASGOW

V

Dunkin' Donuts used to stay open twenty-four hours a day; it doesn't any more. In the mornings and afternoons women, with aching feet and laden with plastic shopping bags crammed with goods from the stores on Argyle Street, use it as a haven of rest, easing their swollen feet out of tight shoes, taking tea or coffee, and gossiping. In the early evening young couples gather there on their way from work, deciding what to do with themselves for the evening, exchanging jokes and laughing a great deal, but brittlely, exchanging words of love too, the girls doe-eyed, their young men cocky.

It was in the hours after midnight, when all those who had homes had gone to them, that Dunkin' Donuts became a meeting-place and temporary shelter for the young homeless. They lingered long over cups of milky coffee or beakers of cola, grateful for the warmth, and for the strange consolation they derived from seeing others in the same predicament as themselves. Many were regulars and the staff knew them, calling them by their first names, cheering them up without even knowing it. Any stranger was watched, covertly but carefully, regarded as a possible danger if not an outright enemy, yet somehow those watchful eyes seemed to convey the idea that he would always be given the benefit of the doubt.

The fact that so many youngsters gathered there made it of interest to the police. They visited it frequently, checking identities, looking

49

for suspects of petty crime, keeping an eye out for drugs. Of course, these police visits alarmed and perturbed the proprietors. It gave the café a bad name, gave it a reputation they would have preferred it didn't have. So they decided not to stay open twenty-four hours. They closed it at midnight, and for a few hours before that they put a doorman just inside, with instructions to keep out the undesirables. The homeless have gone elsewhere.

But Dunkin' Donuts was still an all-nighter when Jimmy went there, and felt those shrewd eyes on him as he took his coffee from the counter and made his way to a table by the window. Yet, when he looked up and glanced casually about, no one appeared to be the least interested in him: nobody stared at him, nobody, for the moment, made any attempt to make contact with him. But he sensed they were talking about him, asking themselves what had put him on the street.

His cup was very full, and he lowered his head to sip:

—Please don't do that, James, Mum said. Bring the cup to your lips, not your face down to the cup. It's *very* vulgar.

—Better than having him slop it all over the place, Dad said, defending him, and giving him a smile with his eyes.

—That's not the point, Mum said.

'Anyone here?'

'Jimmy looked up.

'Anyone sitting here?'

Jimmy shook his head. 'No,' he said, and watched the boy sit down opposite him. He was older than Jimmy, about nineteen, slim and pinched, with one eye that had a cast in it, making it stare. His dark hair was gelled and spiky, his hands dirty and restless. 'Haven't seen you here before,' he said.

'Haven't been here before.'

'That's why I haven't seen you then.'

'Must be.'

'I'm Glenn.'

'Jimmy.'

'Where you from?'

'Why?'

'Just asking.'

'Dundee.'

'Dundee!' Glenn feigned horror. 'Been there once. Once was enough. Right shit-hole Dundee is.' He grinned, showing uneven yellow teeth with food padding the crevices. 'Only joking. No worse than anywhere else in this shitty world, I suppose.' He reached in his pocket and pulled out a half-smoked cigarette. He lit it with a green disposable lighter, cocking his head to one side, and inhaled deeply. Then he offered it to Jimmy. 'Want a draw?'

Jimmy shook his head.

'Don't smoke?'

Jimmy shook his head again.

'Lucky you.'

Jimmy shrugged.

'Every penny I get goes on these things.' He looked hard at Jimmy from under his eyelids. 'Don't suppose you've got enough to get me a coke, have you, pal?'

Without a word Jimmy pushed a pound coin across the table. 'Thanks, pal,' Glenn said, pouncing on the coin, and left the table. By the time he had reached the counter another boy had come to the table and sat down, sliding into the seat. He was pale with reddish-brown hair that had been streaked. His teeth protruded a little and Jimmy could tell he was conscious of these since the boy kept running his tongue over them, and tried to keep his lips over them. He jerked his head towards Glenn's back. 'He been bothering you?' he asked.

'No.'

'Bummin' off you though, wasn't he?'

Jimmy shrugged. 'Just for a coke.'

'That's for starters. Got to watch yourself in here. Don't go handing over money to every shit-face that asks. Got to be hard. Tell them you're not a fucking charity.'

'Okay.'

'I mean it. The first thing you've got to learn is to look after number one. Nobody else will.'

Jimmy nodded.

'Where you from?'

Jimmy sighed. 'Dundee.'

'Just get in?'

Jimmy nodded.

'Got somewhere to sleep?'

'Course I have. Going to stay with my grandparents.'

The boy grinned. 'Oh. Your grandparents, eh? That's nice. And where do they live?'

Jimmy could feel his face redden. He looked towards the counter and saw Glenn turn, saw his face cloud in anger when he noticed his place had been usurped, saw him slouch to another table and sit down sullenly. 'Why you want to know that?'

The boy widened his grin. 'Yeah, you're right. None of my damn business. Just thought you might need somewhere to kip. I know what it's like.'

Jimmy stared at him.

The boy stared back.

'Know what what's like?' Jimmy asked.

'It's shit having to admit you've nowhere to go,' the boy told him seriously. 'And that no one gives a toss about you, ain't it?' He looked out the window, and spoke to his reflection. 'We all of us did the same thing, you know. I did, anyway, when I first got here. From Aberdeen. Pretended I was okay. That I didn't need anyone's help. By the way,' he said, turning back to face Jimmy, 'I'm Dave.' He held out his hand.

'Jimmy,' Jimmy said, and shook hands.

'Well, Jimmy from Dundee, you won't survive by yourself. Not in Glasgow anyway. If the police don't lift you and charge you with some burglary they haven't been able to solve, the muggers will have a go. Or the sneak thieves. They're the worst. Right bastards. Strip you naked while you're asleep and you won't notice a thing until you wake up in the morning with your balls frozen. Of course, if you really *do* have grandparents to go to—'

'I don't,' Jimmy admitted.

'Didn't think so. Anyone?'

Jimmy shook his head.

'A wee orphan like myself,' Dave told him, and laughed ruefully. 'Got any money left?'

Jimmy stiffened. 'A bit.'

'Don't worry—I'm not going to ask you for any of it. Just want to warn you to watch out for it. Don't do daft things like putting it in your shoe or anything. That's the first place the muggers look. They know that one. Best thing is get a wee plastic bag and tape the lot between your legs.'

Jimmy nodded.

'No one's likely to get it from there without your noticing it.'

'No.'

'You get the buroo?'

'The what?'

'The buroo. A giro. Income Support.'

'Never heard of it.'

'Oh, shit. How old are you?'

'Sixteen.'

Dave gave him a sideways look. 'Sure?'

'Sure I'm sure.'

'You don't look it.'

'I'm sixteen.'

'Okay. Okay. Well, then, you're in the shit, mate. You can't get Income Support for a couple of years. You might be able to get a crisis loan but that's not for certain. You're going to have to make your money last as long as you can—not buy cokes for creeps like that,' Dave advised, jerking his head towards Glenn.

'I only gave him a pound.'

'Ha! Jesus! A pound! You gave that dick-head a pound? That'd keep most of us in food for a couple of days. Two bags of chips. One a day.'

'Some food.'

'It's food—that's what counts. We're not great ones for quality, you know.'

'Like being an orphan,' Jimmy tells Miss Pimm, and smiles to himself as he sees her eyes soften into motherly sympathy as she ponders the answer to her question, What did it feel like to find yourself all alone in a strange city? 'Did you have any money?'

'Some.'

'How much?'

'A few quid. About sixty.'

'Ah,' sighs Miss Pimm as if that answer relieves her considerably. 'So you were able to get somewhere to stay?'

'Oh, yes.'

'A bed and breakfast?'

'Something like that.'

He treats this house like an hotel, Mum complained.

Boys do, Dad explained.

But he never brings any of his friends home.

Dad said nothing.

Doesn't he have any?

I'm sure he has.

You'd think he was ashamed of us or something.

Dad stayed quiet.

Or that he was afraid to bring them here, Mum added.

Don't be so ridiculous, Alice, Dad snapped.

Well, I don't like it, Mum said.

Dad closed his eyes.

'I know somewhere we can sleep—if you're interested,' Dave told Jimmy, adding quickly, 'I'm not trying to push you or anything. If you've sorted something out for yourself, that's okay.'

'I haven't. Thanks.'

'We better get going soon, then. Places fill up pretty quick. It's just a squat, but it's a good one. Safe. Out in Maryhill.'

'I'm ready when you are.'

'Right. Let's go.'

They stood up and made for the door. Behind them someone gave a lewd whistle, and a couple of youngsters tittered. Dave turned and glared, and the sniggering stopped.

Now that he was standing, Dave looked a lot shorter than he had appeared when seated. He was a stocky young man with thick legs and arms. His eyes were small and bright and pale blue, and his nose was flat as though it might have been broken once. Above one eye there was a small jagged scar that cut into the eyebrow, severing it. 'Ignore them,' he said.

Outside the wind hurtled up from the river sending junk-food cartons scudding along the pavement. A drunk approached them, begging. 'Piss off,' Dave said harshly. 'I can't stand beggars,' he told Jimmy as they walked along. 'That's one thing I've never done, although lots of kids do. Make good money too, if they're clever at it. Sooner steal, I would, than go round begging off people. Really degrading that is, I think.'

Jimmy nodded.

They plodded on, shoulders hunched against the wind. 'I was going to meet someone in George Square,' Dave said. 'But let's avoid it.'

From across the street someone called, 'Dave!' and a young boy with bright red hair and an acned face came diving through the traffic.

'Oh, shit,' Dave muttered.

'Hi, Dave,' the youngster said.

'What *you* want, Ally?'

'Got any—' Ally began, and then paused, giving Jimmy a suspicious look. 'You know, any—'

'No,' Dave said.

'Got a fag then?'

'Smoking's bad for your health.'

Ally gave a huge grin. 'Yeah, I know. Good though, eh? Heard this one—what's the difference between a Rottweiler and a social worker?'

'Dunno. What?'

'You can get your kid back off a Rottweiler,' Ally told them, and doubled up with laughter.

Dave laughed too, but he said, 'It's not *that* funny.'

'I thought it was,' Ally said. He was hopping from foot to foot, his hands flapping.

Dave took a ten-pack of cigarettes from his pocket.

'I've got another one,' Ally said, eyeing the cigarettes.

'No thanks,' Dave said quickly, and handed over a cigarette.

'Thanks, pal,' Ally said, sticking the cigarette behind his ear, and dashing off back across the street.

'Who was that?' Jimmy asked.

Dave shrugged. 'Just a kid.'

'Oh,' Jimmy said, and then, as though the thought had just struck him, 'What did you mean—avoid George Square?'

'Two places you've got to avoid in Glasgow, pal. Buchanan Bus Station in the afternoon, and George Square at night. That's where the rent boys and perverts go, and you don't want to get mixed up in any of that shit.'

'What you mean—rent boys?'

'Jesus! You mean you don't know?'

'No.'

Dave stopped suddenly and faced him. 'Christ, you're innocent. Rent boys—they go with queers and have their cocks sucked for money.'

'Oh.'

They walked on, and Dave gave Jimmy a sideways glance, and a wicked grin. 'They'd love you, though. Pretty little laddie that you are.'

'Piss off,' Jimmy said.

'Such language,' Dave said, and then hooted with laughter. 'You're learning. Good.' He slapped Jimmy playfully on the shoulder. 'Seriously—remember what I said and keep away from those places.'

'I will.'

'Do. Lots of lads you meet will try and get you into that racket. They'll tell you it's easy money and all that crap. Sure it's easy money, but it's not worth it.'

'I've got money.'

'Yeah. I know. You've got a few quid *now*. But that'll soon go, and then what?'

Jimmy shrugged.

'That's what I mean. Don't think it's easy to come by—it ain't. All those charitable places *say* they'll help, but when you go to them all they really want to offer is what they call "support". You know what that is, eh? I'll tell you. It's bullshit. Doesn't put food in your belly. And they always start off by saying they understand. That's more bullshit. How the fuck could they understand? You're out in the big wide world now, sunshine, and it's a bastard of a place to be.'

'Thanks a lot.'

It was the best part of an hour before they reached the squat in Maryhill. 'Here we are,' Dave said, crawling through a gap in a corrugated iron fence. 'Pass me your bag.'

Jimmy passed his bag and crawled after it through the gap, waiting while Dave shoved the iron flap back into place. They were in what had once been someone's garden. It was now overgrown with nettles and thistles, and long, tough couch grass. A few climbing roses still struggled up the wall that ran along two sides of the plot, and an old, gnarled apple tree, almost leafless and riddled with disease, leaned awkwardly away from the dilapidated two-storey house. Dave saw Jimmy staring at the tree. 'You know something? A dick-head called Angus—from Skye, he was—called this the Garden of Eden,' he said, and started to laugh wildly. 'Come on.'

Jimmy followed Dave into the house, through an opening that had been the back door. 'This way—mind your step.' A light flickering at the end of the passage lit their way. There was rubble and debris strewn all along the passageway, bits of brick, bed springs, an old fridge. From the room with the light, the sound of *Dark Side of the Moon* came, playing quietly. 'This is it,' he said, a bit apologetic, standing to one side.

It was a large room, larger than Jimmy had expected from the size

57

of the house. It had a high ceiling and two huge windows, both covered with blankets. A candle in a Chianti bottle was on the mantelpiece, but the fireplace was long gone. There was an old armchair, a formica-topped table, and a small gas stove. 'Hi, Pete,' Dave said, and someone on a mattress in the corner grunted. 'That's Pete,' Dave explained. 'He lives here *all* the time. Good bloke. Very into his Pink Floyd and hash. Fussy who he lets in here, that's why there's never any trouble.'

Jimmy peered into the gloom to try and put a face on Pete, but all he could make out was long, unwieldy hair atop a white blob.

'He's our resident film star too,' Dave went on, dumping Jimmy's bag down by the double mattress. 'We'll have to share this—okay?'

Jimmy nodded. 'Okay. What d'you mean—film star?'

Dave giggled. 'Joke,' he said. 'They're always sending up film crews from the telly to talk to us homeless. Very fashionable we are now. Make good viewing we do. And Pete there's a natural.' He giggled again as though remembering something. 'Really knows how to turn on the old sob stories. That's all those bastards want. He tells them all sorts of crap, and they love it.' He lifted a folded blanket from the mattress and shook it, spreading it out. 'He's got the biggest brownest eyes you've ever seen and he sure knows how to use them.'

'Melt your heart, eh?' Jimmy suggested.

'That's it,' Dave agreed, and grinned hugely. 'They even flew him down to London once so he could pretend to be a wee Scots orphan stranded in the dirty big city.'

'Oh.'

'They always pretend they don't pay, but Pete does all right.'

'Oh,' Jimmy said again.

'He must have been in every bloody documentary they've made, and no one seems to have copped on yet.' Suddenly Dave guffaws. 'You should have heard what he told one bitch reporter when she asked him how he managed for sex on the street.'

'What?'

'Said he cut a wee hole in a melon and used that.'

Jimmy laughed.

'And she believed him. "But that's awful," she said,' Dave mimicked. 'And Pete said, "No, it's really terrific".'

'Jesus.'

58

'They didn't use it though.'

'Not surprised.'

'They're right thicks.'

'You ever been in one?'

Dave shook his head. 'Naw. Not interested.'

Under one of the windows a bundle stirred. 'That you, Dave?' a voice asked.

'Yeah, it's me,' Dave answered. Then, in a whisper, he told Jimmy, 'That's Graham from Dumfries. Only been here a month but he seems okay. His Dad's a real drunk and beats the shit out of him every night. You should see the poor bastard's back. Like Christ crucified, it is. He's been in one of those films too. Anyone can be in them if you say what they want. Plenty of juicy crap, that's what they like. Drugs and drink and a bit of the old prostitution, they love that. They don't really give a shit about us as long as the telly makes *them* look good.' He laughed wryly. 'Funny thing is, they think *they're* fooling *us*. Stupid bastards.'

'Who's that with you?' Graham wanted to know.

'Mate of mine from Dundee,' Dave said. 'Known him ages. He's fine. Don't worry, pal.'

'Oh,' Graham managed, and then went back to sleep.

'He always asks that when someone new comes in. Scared stiff it might be someone violent,' Dave explained to Jimmy. 'He's a really gentle person and violence scares the hell out of him. Even when he sees it on telly he starts to shake. Even seen him crying when someone's getting beaten up.' He flopped down on the mattress. 'Come on,' he said, patting the mattress. 'Don't worry. You're dead safe.'

Jimmy lay down on the mattress beside Dave, and turned his face to the wall, breathing as quietly as he could. The candle flickered and made ghoulish patterns on the wall by his head. He closed his eyes quickly.

'Try and get a really good sleep,' Dave advised. 'You never know but this place might not be here tomorrow.'

'What?'

'Might not be here,' Dave said again. 'It's due for demolition. They could come and knock it down in the morning.'

'Then where do we sleep?'

Dave gave a small snort. 'Find somewhere else, of course.'
'Oh.'
'Don't worry. There's plenty of squats around. I'll look after you.'
'Oh.'
'Welcome to the world of the homeless, pal.'
'Some world.'
'It's not that bad when you get used to it.'
'No?'
'And you can get used to anything,' Dave said. Then he added with a little laugh, 'You'll probably have to.'

They lay there, side by side, for some time listening to the Pink Floyd music coming from Pete's battered tape machine. The candle flickered in the draught, continuing its monstrous artistry.

Oh, what a shame, Mum said. You don't get your wish.
Why not, Mum?
Well, you didn't blow out all the candles on your cake in one go. You have to do it in one puff or your wish isn't granted.
Don't be silly, Alice, Dad said. Of course he gets his wish.
That's not the way I was told it.
Well, it's the way *I* was told it, and it's the way Jimmy's going to have it. Anything Jimmy wants he can have, Dad added.
You spoil him so, Cameron.
I like to spoil him, Dad said.
It's not good for him.
Nonsense.

After a while Dave turned and threw one arm about Jimmy. Instantly Jimmy stiffened, and Dave withdrew his arm quickly. 'Sorry,' he whispered. 'I didn't mean anything. Just thought it might comfort you a bit. Tell you a secret. All I ever wanted was someone to cuddle me. Never had one—a proper cuddle I mean. You don't get cuddles in children's homes. Anyway, all I was going to say was don't worry. It's not all that bad. If you want I'll look after you 'til you get to know your way around.'

Jimmy said nothing.

'You awake?'

'Yes. Thanks for that.'

'No problem.'

'Dave?'

'Yeah?'

'Put your arm around me.'

'Did you not think of telephoning your parents just to let them know you were safe?' Miss Pimm asks.

'Yeah, I thought about it.'

'But you didn't do it?'

'No.'

'Why not?'

'No reason.'

'You must have known they'd be worried.'

'Maybe.'

'Did you want them to worry?'

Jimmy thinks about that for a while. 'Probably,' he admits finally.

'Were you trying to punish them for something?'

'No,' Jimmy says quickly, too quickly, and Miss Pimm makes a little note on her jotter, and Dr Rutherford narrows his beady eyes.

'You sure of that?'

'Yes, I'm sure. Why would I want to punish them?'

'You tell me, Jimmy. You were prepared to upset and worry them.'

'I didn't see it like that.'

'How *did* you see it, Jimmy?'

'I didn't even think about them really. I just wanted to get away by myself. Have some fun,' Jimmy says.

'Great fun this sleeping rough, isn't it?' Dave asked the next morning as he lay on the mattress, his hands folded behind his head, watching Jimmy try to stretch the stiffness from his bones. 'Fashionable too, I hear them saying.'

Jimmy sniffed. 'This place really stinks,' he said, looking about to see if there was a basin in which to wash.

'You ain't smelt nothing yet, pal. You should try some of those hostels they try and get us to stay in. Now they *really* stink. People pissing in their beds and puking up all over each other. What you looking for?'

'Somewhere to wash.'

Dave gave a snorting laugh. 'Nothing here. Water's been cut off. You'll have to make do 'til we get down town. You can wash in the public shit-house at the station.'

'Oh.'

'Anyway, first things first.'

'Like?'

'Food, pal, food. Got to get something into your belly to start the day on.'

'Good. I'm starving.'

'You'll get used to that,' Dave tells him drily.

'Where do we go? That café again?'

Dave burst out laughing. 'And pay for it? Not on your life. Never pay for anything you can get free. Anyway, who's got money?'

'I have. I told you.'

'Yeah. Well, you keep it. Hang on to it. You'll need it soon enough. We have this place we get good nosh free.'

'Where?'

'I'll show you. What you want—Italian or Chinese?' Dave asked, grinning as he got up and ran his fingers through his hair. 'Never mind. You'll see.'

'Can't wait,' Jimmy said.

'Well, let's get going then.'

'What about my bag?'

'Oh, shit! I forgot you had *possessions*.' Dave frowned as he thought for a moment. Then he brightened. 'I know where we can put it. You don't want to be lugging that around with you all day. Attract too much attention. The police will think you've robbed somewhere, and the muggers will be dying to get their shitty fingers on it. Don't want to spend all my time fighting those bastards off. Come on. We'll dump the bag first, and then eat.'

'I don't want to be a—'

'That's okay.'

'You don't *have* to look after me, you know.'

'I know that,' Dave said. 'Tell you what, though, it's nice to have someone to look after.'

Miss Pimm looks at her watch, and says, 'Oh, dear,' to herself, and asks her next question quickly, in clipped tones, as if pressed for time.

'When did you come down here to London, Jimmy?'

'Huh?'

'When did you come to London?'

'Oh, I don't know.'

'Give me some idea.'

'Well, it was much later. About three months ago only.'

'And the other months you were in Glasgow?'

'Yes.'

'All the time?'

'Yea, mostly. Sometimes we went to Edinburgh for a few days.'

'We?'

'Me.'

'You said we.'

'I meant me.'

'You didn't make any friends?'

'No.'

'None?'

'Not really.'

Miss Pimm looks surprised. 'That surprises me.'

'I knew people, but they weren't what you'd call friends.'

'What would you call them?'

Jimmy decides to ignore that question.

'Can you give me the names of some of the people you knew—even if they weren't what I'd call friends?'

'Why?'

'Just—well, just for the record.'

Jimmy shrugs. 'We didn't often give names.'

'But sometimes you did.'

'Sometimes.'

'Well?'

'Oh, Angus and Graham and Brian and Joe.'

'No last names?'

'No last names.'

'Never give no one your last name,' Dave warned. 'And don't carry anything on you that has your last name on it. No letters or anything.'

'Why not?'

''Cause it's the only thing you've got that's your own, and you don't want just anyone knowing it.'

'Oh. And what happens if I get killed?'

'What d'you mean?'

'They won't know who I am.'

'No. And they won't care either, pal. They'll be only too glad to stick you in the ground and bring the homeless problem down by one.'

'You're a cynic.'

They had left Jimmy's hold-all at the YMCA for safe keeping, and were making their way back into the centre of the city. 'Dave, I'm gasping. Can't we stop for coffee or something?'

'Food first. We're nearly there.'

'I'll treat you,' Jimmy said, trying to tempt his new pal.

'You'll have to treat me anyway, but later. We're just there.'

'Where?'

They turned a corner and started down a narrow alley. 'There,' Dave said triumphantly. 'Right over there.'

Right over there proved to be the back door of a takeaway café. A number of young people had already gathered outside, waiting. They eyed Dave and Jimmy with hostility until one of them recognised Dave, and said, 'Hiya.'

'Hiya,' Dave answered, and everyone relaxed, and went back to the monotonous pastime of waiting, shuffling their feet, some walking in small, tight circles, silent. Then the bolt of the door was pulled back, and everyone tensed before moving towards it. Their eyes brightened. One or two of the youngsters licked saliva from their lips.

The door opened and a man came out, carrying a huge, metal cooking tray, the sort Italians use for enormous lasagnes. But there was nothing Italian about the man: he was thin as a rake, with wispy blond hair going grey. He was tall and morose, and his pale blue eyes watered, the tears settling in heavy black bags under his eyes. He shoved the tray on to a stack of cardboard boxes, and stood back, watching, in much the same way as a lion-keeper might watch his charges—with fascination and a little fear.

'That's your breakfast,' Dave whispered.

'That's it,' the man said.

Jimmy stared in disgust at the tray. It was piled high with food, left-overs, jumbled together: lasagne, spaghetti, chips, rice, ravioli, and a mixture of vegetables.

'Good, eh?' Dave asked enthusiastically.

'I can't eat *that*,' Jimmy said, feeling his stomach heave.

'Why not?'

'It's disgusting, that's why.'

'It's food, pal. That's what it is—food. And it's *free.*'

'It's shit.'

Dave looked surprised and hurt. He looked as if he had prepared the food himself and had it rejected. Then he shrugged, and walked away from Jimmy, walked towards the food and started shoving the mixture into his mouth.

Eat your cabbage, James, Mum said.

I can't.

It's good for you.

It tastes like—

Don't you dare say what I think you're going to say, Mum interrupted quickly. I'll not have any of *that* language in this house. You should be grateful for any food you get. Think of all those poor Ethiopians starving.

Oh, for goodness sake, Alice, Dad exclaimed. Please don't drag your starving millions into every conversation. Jimmy's cabbage wouldn't make a damn bit of difference to them, and you know it. It's so illogical.

That's not the point.

Come to think of it, Dad went on, they probably wouldn't eat it either. He winked at Jimmy, and Mum fell silent. But she had noticed the conspiratorial wink, and smiled to herself with her eyes. It really pleased her to see a father and son get on so well, but that was before Jimmy had made his accusation.

'Sure you don't want some?' Dave called.

Jimmy shook his head.

'Please yourself.'
Jimmy watched them eat.

And another time:
What in heaven's name is the matter with you, James? Speak to him,
Cameron, will you?
Dad looked blankly up from his plate.
He won't eat anything, Mum complained. Just look at him. All he
does is nibble a couple of mouthfuls and then shove the rest of his
food about his plate.
Aren't you hungry? Dad asked.
Jimmy shook his head.
He's not hungry, Dad said in a matter-of-fact way.
Well, are you sick? Mum demanded.
Jimmy shook his head again.
He's simply not hungry, Alice, Dad said, wanting to get the conver-
sation over and done with. He always got edgy when Mum questioned
Jimmy, just in case something might come out.
Well, it's just not normal, Mum said. A young man like him with no
appetite. Most boys his age eat like horses. *Something's* putting him
off his food, and I want to know what it is.
Don't be silly, Alice. Please, Dad said. He's told you—he's just not
hungry.

'You not eating?' the man asked Jimmy.
    Jimmy shook his head.
    'Not good enough for you, eh?'
    'Not hungry,' Jimmy said.

'He's eaten already,' Dave called.

'Oh,' the man said.

'Just not hungry,' Dave explained. 'Wait 'til he is, and he'll eat the whole tray by himself.'

The man nodded.

'*Now* can we get some coffee?' Jimmy demanded.

'Sure,' Dave told him.

'How could you eat that shit!'

'Nothing wrong with it.'

'It's what other people left.'

'So?'

'It's the crap they throw out.'

'So?'

'Don't keep saying "so".'

'Yeah, well I'll remind you of all this in a few days when your money's run out, and your belly starts shrinking.'

'You'll never catch me eating that crap.'

'Beggars can't be choosers.'

'I'd sooner starve.'

'Want to bet? Tell you one thing—that grub was better than most stuff we have to eat to survive. Wait 'til you have to start eating *real* rubbish, from rubbish bins, then you can really start whining.'

Miss Pimm has decided she has asked enough questions for one day. 'Well, Jimmy, I think that's enough for one day, don't you?'

Jimmy says nothing.

'Yes, well, I think it is. But we'll have to go on with it tomorrow,' she says brightly, making it sound like a treat. 'And tomorrow I'm going to ask you about the rest of your time in Glasgow, and maybe about London if we've time. All right?'

Jimmy made a small grimace. 'Sure.'

'Good. You might think about it all tonight, will you?'

Jimmy nods.

'Fine. Well, we'd better be going.' Miss Pimm stands up. 'Unless— unless you have something to ask Jimmy, have you?' she asks Dr Rutherford who has unwound his legs and stood up also.

But Dr Rutherford has nothing he wants to ask Jimmy, it seems. He shakes his head. 'I'd better take the lighter, hadn't I?' he asks Miss Pimm.

'Oh. Oh, yes. And I'd better have the cigarettes, Jimmy. I'm sorry. I'll bring them again tomorrow, though.'

Jimmy nods.

'Until tomorrow then. 'Bye Jimmy.'

''Bye.'

VI

The same constable, this time in shirt-sleeves, brings in his tea. There's a long, fat sausage, a slice of bread and margarine, and another mug of strong, sweet tea.

'You do all the work round here?' Jimmy asks. The constable grins. 'Seems like it. Get that inside you and you'll feel better,' he says. And then he adds with a friendly enough smile, 'Not *much* better, mind, but a bit.'

'Thanks,' Jimmy says.

'There's a message for you too.'

Jimmy looks up.

'Your parents will be here first thing in the morning.'

'Oh.'

'I thought you'd be pleased.'

'Bloody thrilled.'

'Don't get on, eh?'

'You could say that.'

'That why you left home?'

Jimmy chews on his sausage. 'Yeah.' Then he looks up with a slight grin although his eyes have narrowed. 'You the good guy or something?' he asks.

'Sorry?'

'That's how you work it, isn't it? Send in the good guy to soften me up and then if you don't get what you want you send in the tough one—the one who shouts and says he'll beat the shit out of me.'

'You've been watching too many old films,' the policeman says.

'Oh, yeah? I've had mates brought in by you lot. I've heard things, you know.'

'I bet you have.'

'So, are you the good guy?'

The constable puts a foot on the bunk bed, and leans his elbow on it. 'I'm just trying to be civil with you,' he says quietly. 'Half the young toe-rags we get in here need to be bashed about a bit before they get sense.'

'So when do you start on me?'

'You a toe-rag?'

Jimmy shrugs.

The constable glances towards the door, and then leans forward a bit. 'We already know a lot more about all this than you think,' he confides.

'Clever,' Jimmy says.

'No,' the policeman says. 'Not clever. Just—' He shrugs, and stands upright. 'No one's going to batter you. Not unless you step out of line. Which you won't.'

'Won't I?'

The constable shakes his head. 'Not the sort.' He makes a move towards the door. Turning suddenly, he asks, 'Rough on you, were they?'

'Who?'

'Parents.'

Jimmy looks up and stares him straight in the eyes. 'No,' he says, and looks quickly away again.

The constable hesitates in case Jimmy wants to add something, and then, as Jimmy remains silent, he adds, 'Well, don't worry. There'll be somebody with you all the time—all during the visit.'

'I see.'

The constable opens the door.

'I don't *have* to see them, do I?'

'No. Not if you don't want to.'

Jimmy nods. 'Okay.'

'I would though, if I were you. Get it over with. My guess is they're just checking you're all right—like you say, just checking we haven't bashed you about,' the constable says with a wicked grimace.

'Yeah.'

'Doctor, isn't he? Your Dad.'

'Yep.'

'They're the worst. Them and solicitors.'

'Worst for what?'

'Causing us trouble.'

'Oh.'

'Can't ever believe *their* kids can get into trouble.'

'Oh.'

The constable sighs. 'Anyway, drink your tea, and then try and get some kip.'

'I'll try.'

'That's all any of us can do, lad. Try.'

Let *me* try, Dad said. Jimmy was about six. A small red pimple, irritating and bleeding, had developed low down on his spine. Mum had given him ointment, TCP, to put on it, but the spot was awkward to get at. Dad took the ointment, squeezed some on to his finger and rubbed it on the spot, placing his free hand on Jimmy's belly to hold him steady. He took a very long time about applying it, and as he smeared the ointment the fingers of his other hand flicked down on to Jimmy's tiny penis. And the treatment over, Dad fondled Jimmy's buttocks, squeezing them playfully. Then he kissed his bottom, saying quietly, 'That will make it better.' That was the first time he had done anything as far as Jimmy could remember, but he checked the pimple regularly for several nights, each time fondling and kissing him.

'Do *try* and concentrate,' Mum said wearily, but Jimmy cannot remember when or what the occasion was.

Then she turned to Dad. 'I don't know what's coming over this boy. All of a sudden he's so—so *vague* about everything. Doesn't seem to listen to a thing I say. Always thinking about something else. Daydreaming.'

Dad decided to make a joke of it. 'I don't always listen to what you say, dear,' he said.

'You don't have to tell me *that*,' Mum snapped.

But Dad probably did listen to everything Mum said although he often chose to ignore her. It wasn't that she said silly things, but often her opinions were, well, old-fashioned and they sounded pompous. Mum was from a very good family in Perthshire, a very wealthy family, and she had been pampered and cosseted until she got married. Indeed, much of what she said wasn't of her own thinking, just views that had been impressed upon her as a child, and she clung to them in much the same way as she might have clung to a favourite doll had she had one, as though she needed them to remind her of happier, fast-fading times. And despite Dad's position, despite, too, the fact that she was proud of his medical prowess, she sometimes told herself that she had married beneath her, consoling herself that her sacrifice would be rewarded in some vague way. Sometimes, when angry, she would call up some extraordinary word and include it in her reproach of Dad. And when Dad looked bemused she would say, a bit haughtily, 'It's a perfectly ordinary English word. If you can't understand it, Cameron, it just demonstrates the difference in our educations.'

So Dad often ignored her, and this verbal rebuff had spread over the years into their physical relationship. They seldom touched each other now, and when they did—usually in the form of a swift kiss on the cheek and more often than not in public—it was perfunctory.

From time to time there had been rumours that Dad had been having a relationship with some other woman, but these were never proved, never even pursued by Mum since, in a way, she was content that they might happen as long as he was discreet, and as long as he maintained the image of a good husband and father. Image was important to Mum. Dad once told her, 'You know, Alice, I honestly believe you'd tolerate anything as long as it didn't tarnish the image you have of yourself.' But he regretted making his observation when Mum snapped back, 'Yes, well I've had to, haven't I, Cameron. My tolerance has saved you a lot of—'

'All right, dear,' Dad said quickly.

'Try it,' Dave said.

They had been together in Glasgow for nearly two months when Dave offered him the joint.

'It's drugs,' Jimmy said.

'Only hash. Won't do you any harm. Honest. Just make you feel calm.'

It was Sunday morning and they had come down to the station for no particular reason. They stood by the telephones, ready to pick up a phone and pretend to be talking if any police came along. The tiled floor was damp and people slithered about, one young man in trainers falling as his feet went from under him. That made them laugh, but not for long. The hamburger place was closed, but the smell of meat and onions still hung about the entrance, and that made them feel hungry.

'I am calm,' Jimmy said.

'Well, calmer.'

'I'm just hungry,' Jimmy complained.

'This'll stop you feeling hungry. It's not like the hard stuff. I'd never let you take the hard stuff.'

'Graham does.'

'Graham's a mess. Has been ever since he was a kid. His dad injected him with heroin when he was eight.'

'Shit.'

'They asked him in court why he did it. You know what the bastard said to that?'

'What?'

'Did it for a laugh, he said.'

'Shit.'

74

'Some laugh, eh?'

'Shit.'

Two teenage girls hurried into the station and stood staring up at the huge electronic noticeboard. They looked like students, and giggled a lot.

'Wow,' Dave said, 'She's bonny.'

'Who?'

'That one there. The one with the long blonde hair.'

'Oh. Yeah. She's all right.'

'She's really bonny,' Dave insisted. 'That's the sort of lassie I'm going to have when I get myself settled down.' His voice turned wistful. 'Must be great that. Having your own place and your own girl, and kids. You want kids?'

'Hadn't thought about it.'

'I do. Four of them. All my own.'

'That all?'

'It's enough,' Dave said, taking Jimmy's sarcastic remark seriously. 'That's what I dream about. Having my own family and looking after them. Must be really great that,' he said again. 'Coming home and having them run out to meet you and throw their little arms about you, and call you Dad.'

'You're mad.'

'No, I'm not. Got to dream, pal. There's not much else we can do. But I'll make it happen, just you see if I don't. Be best man if you like.'

'Thanks.'

'Hey, that *would* be cool. Me getting married and you being best man.'

Jimmy gave him a sceptical look.

'You want this or not?' Dave asked, offering the joint. 'There's only a couple of drags left. Can't waste it.'

'Okay.'

'You'll see, it'll make you relax, that's all.'

Try to relax, Dad whispered. I'm only doing this because I love you, he said, holding Jimmy close, and placing his penis between his legs, moving back and forth.

And then a few weeks later, maybe seven weeks, Dad said, We'll try something different tonight, something to bring us really close, and he rubbed vaseline on Jimmy's rectum and tried to force his penis inside. But Jimmy squirmed and screamed, and Dad said, All right, all right. We won't do that, and he went back to the old way, putting his penis between Jimmy's legs, and thumping away until he had finished. He bought Jimmy a CD player the next day.

Try as he might, and he tries hard, Jimmy cannot sleep. The curious feeling of security the tiny cell had given him earlier has gone, and now, for the first time, he feels frightened and totally alone. He does manage to doze from time to time, but always wakes with a start, sitting up instantly, wondering for a second where he is, listening. He can hear noises from outside the police station. A dog barking forlornly—No, dear, we most certainly *cannot* have a dog, Mum said. They're dirty creatures. They leave their hair everywhere, and I know who would end up having to clean up after the beast; a radio playing what sounds like Jason Donovan—How you can listen to such rubbish, I just don't know, Mum said. It's not even music, just wailing as far as I can tell; someone shouting, someone else cursing, but those curses seem to come from another cell.

'Sure I've been inside,' Dave admitted.

They had left the station and now walked along the river. They made this walk often. There was something about the water that drew them although they both admitted to a dread of the grey coldness, admitted, too, that it must be terrible to drown.

'Not prison or anything,' Dave went on. 'Just banged up in a police cell for a night or two. Then up in front of the sheriff who dishes out this fine he knows I can't pay.'

'What for?'

'Got to give me something, doesn't he?'

'I meant what were you banged up for?'

'Oh. Just shoplifting and stuff. Getting food. Ham and things. Great the way they put that meat in little packets. Just right for slipping under your coat.'

'Not that great.'

'—?'

'You got caught, didn't you?'

'Only a couple of times.'

'I'd hate to be locked up.'

'Nothing to it. All you have to do is get your head down and sleep. They don't bother you. The police. They know the score.'

'Still wouldn't like it.'

'Nobody *likes* it, stupid. It just happens. Maybe it won't to you.'

'I bloody hope not.'

Jimmy, what has *happened* to you lately?

Mr Corrigan, the maths teacher, was concerned. He had called Jimmy into his office after school, and now sat with his buttocks resting on the edge of his desk, staring over his spectacles. Your work has deteriorated at an alarming rate over the past few months. Is something troubling you, lad? he asks. Is there a problem?

No, Mr Corrigan.

Are you being bullied?

No, Mr Corrigan.

You can tell me in complete confidence, you know. No one will ever know that you did tell me.

I'm not being bullied, Mr Corrigan.

Well, something's the matter. You used to be so good at maths. One of my very best. But now . . . Am I going too fast for you?

Jimmy shook his head. No, Mr Corrigan.

Mr Corrigan sighed. Well, try a bit harder then, will you please?

Yes, Mr Corrigan.

And Jimmy, Mr Corrigan added as Jimmy was about to leave the room. If there ever is something you want to tell me about—

There isn't, Mr Corrigan.

No, but if there ever is—

Thanks, Mr Corrigan.

The flap on the spy-hole of the cell opens, and a single eye peers in. Then the little door set in the main door opens, and a voice asks, 'Are you all right?'

'Yes.'

The little door closes again, quietly, and footsteps pad away along the corridor, pausing at each cell, each little door is opened, each inmate checked.

Dad always closed the bedroom door quietly behind him when he left and made his way back to his own room, his bare feet padding on the polished wooden floor of the landing. For some reason that frightened Jimmy. It wasn't right for Dad to be so secretive and go sneaking about the place. And he was stealthy too when he came into the room and slipped into bed beside Jimmy, always saying, Hush, it's only me.

'I had a brainwave last night,' Dave said.

'Another one?'

'Yeah. How's about you and me going to London?'

'London?'

'Yeah. Always wanted to go to London but never felt like going down there on my own.'

'I've been to London.'

'Yeah? You have? What's it like?'

Jimmy shrugged. 'All right, I suppose. Went with my dad.'

'Lucky bastard. I wish I'd had a dad to take me to London.'

They had just finished supper when Dad said, I've got a treat for you, Jimmy.

Jimmy looked at him.

I've got to go to London for a two-day conference, and I thought I'd take you with me.

Now, James, Mum said. What do you think of *that*?

Jimmy said nothing.

Aren't you thrilled?

Are you coming too? Jimmy asked Mum.

No, Dad said quickly. Just you and me.

Mum gave a silly, girlish giggle. You wouldn't want me there too, she said. Much better for you two men to go off together, she added. I'd only get in the way.

Mum had this thing about calling Jimmy 'a man'. Even before he could walk she called him her 'little man'.

I thought you'd be pleased, Dad said.

Of course he's pleased, Mum answered for him. Aren't you, James?

Yes, Jimmy said quietly.

You see? Mum said to Dad. Of course he's pleased. What son wouldn't be, I ask you?

'That's something I'm always thinking about,' Dave confided.

'What?'

'Having a dad and going places with him. Just having one to talk to. You talk much to your dad?'

'Some. Not much.'

Dave shook his head. 'I would have,' he said.

'You only think you would.'

'Oh, no. I definitely would have. Made sure I did.'

'Depends on what sort of dad you've got, doesn't it?'

Dave gave him a quizzical look. 'Yours sounds all right to me.'

'Oh, great.'

'A bastard, is he?' It was the first time Dave had ever made any comment or asked any question about Jimmy's parents. Indeed, the only thing he knew was that there had been some vague misunderstanding in Dundee.

'Drink, does he?' Dave asked.

'No. Very little anyway.'

'Oh,' Dave said as if he now understood.

'What happened to yours?'

'Pissed off, didn't he. With another woman. Some slag, my mam called her. My mam was the slag though. Always having it off. So, what about London—still want to go?'

'Why not?'

'Let's go then.'

And: Let's go then, Dad said, holding the car door open for Jimmy to climb in. I'll phone you tonight, Alice. Just to let you know we've arrived safely.

Yes, do that, dear. Have a lovely time. And James, do behave yourself. Don't cause your father any trouble.

He won't, Dad said.

Dad was always doing that, answering on his behalf like he was afraid what he might say for himself. Mum did it too.

And send me a postcard, James, Mum said.

Of course he will, Dad told her.

Postcard! Dad snorted as he steered the car out on to the road. You'd think we were off for a couple of months instead of two days. Women! He glanced at Jimmy and chuckled. Better fasten your seat-belt.

You remember Dr Gasgoigne, don't you Jimmy? Dad asked.

Yes, Jimmy answered.

Well, Mrs Gasgoigne is going to show you the sights while I'm at the conference.

Oh.

And when Mrs Gasgoigne brought him back to the hotel Dad wanted to know, I hope he behaved himself, did he?

He was wonderful, Mrs Gasgoigne enthused. Simply wonderful, she added, and Dad looked relieved as she came up to him and kissed him lightly on the cheek. I just wish *my* two boys were as well behaved. He's so *quiet*, she concluded.

He's shy, Dad explained.

Yes, Mrs Gasgoigne agreed. But so bright and interested in everything.

Yes, Dad said.

And later, alone in the hotel room, Dad said, I'm glad you behaved yourself. Then he yawned and stretched. I ate too much, he admitted, and started undressing. And drank too much, he added with a little laugh.

Jimmy was already in bed. He made no reply. He hoped Dad would leave him alone.

Dad went to the bathroom and brushed his teeth. He gargled, spitting a lot. Then he urinated, humming to himself for a while. It's really nice being alone with you, Jimmy, he called. Not having Mum telling us what to do.

Jimmy said nothing. He knew what Dad was doing now. He was brushing his hair with the two ivory-backed hairbrushes that had been his father's. Dad was like that, very particular about his appearance.

Always neat and tidy. Dapper, Mum called it, and to help him she ironed all his shirts, putting just the right amount of starch in the collars, since the laundries nowadays made such a poor job of things. She ironed his underclothes too, and polished his shoes, and his suits were whisked away to the cleaners after only two wearings. She chose his ties; there was always one for his birthday, and probably one for Christmas too. Nice, plain, conservative ties that befitted his standing as a medical man. I really cannot stand those dreadful gaudy things they sell in that new Tie Rack place, she complained once. They look like bits of curtain chopped down.

Jimmy heard Dad put the brushes back into their little leather case, and pull the zip closed. He'd be looking at himself now. Pulling up his lips to examine his teeth, peering at his eyebrows to make sure there were no long, straggly hairs, looking for hairs in his nose too.

And then Dad got in beside him, naked, holding him tightly, the smell of his mouthwash like peppermint. Relax, Jimmy, Dad whispered. He had forgotten the vaseline so he used spittle. Relax, he said again, making it sound more like an order because of its urgency. I won't hurt you.

But it did hurt. Terribly. And as Dad forced himself inside, Jimmy let out one fearful scream before Dad clamped his hand over his mouth.

Jimmy wakes with a start, waking and sitting bolt upright at the same time. A strange policeman in shirt-sleeves is standing over him. 'Hey, hey, hey,' he is saying.

Jimmy blinks.

'Thought you were being murdered,' the policeman says.

'What?'

'Screaming like that. You all right?'

'Yeah. Yeah. Must have been a dream.'

'Must have been one hell of a nightmare, you mean,' the policeman tells him. 'Sure you're okay?'

'Yeah. I'm okay now.'

''Night then.'

'What time is it?'

The policeman checks his watch. 'Just after three. You've still got a few hours left. Make the most of it.' He leaves the cell, closing the door behind him without too much of a bang, but the keys rattle loudly in the stillness.

Jimmy lies back on the bunk, and pulls the grey, coarse blanket up to his chin, shaking.

And did you have a wonderful time? Mum wanted to know.

We certainly did, Dad told her.

Did you see all the sights?

He did.

Buckingham Palace, and the Tower, and the Houses of Parliament?

He saw everything, Dad explained. Mrs Gasgoigne took him everywhere.

Aren't you the lucky young man, Mum said proudly.

He knows he is, Alice, Dad said. Don't you, Jimmy?

Jimmy nodded.

Show Mum what I bought you.

Spoiling him again, Cameron, Mum said before she'd seen anything.

VII

Miss Pimm is already waiting for him as he is escorted back to the interview room the next morning. Dr Rutherford is there too, and both of them seem fidgety and a bit tense. 'Good morning, Jimmy,' Miss Pimm says, but her voice is hoarse and the words don't sound right. She gives a short cough and says, 'Good morning, Jimmy,' again.

Jimmy nods, and sits down.

Dr Rutherford nods, and grunts something, clasping his long fingers about one knee, swinging his foot.

Jimmy nods to him also, and sits down at the table, opposite Miss Pimm. He flicks his eyes about the drab room. It has been cleaned, and the dead wasp is gone. There is the faint smell of disinfectant, or of some cheap polish that could have contained germ-killer.

'Did you sleep all right?' Miss Pimm would like to know.

Jimmy makes a so-so face, and glances significantly at Miss Pimm's handbag. He gives a small smile, and raises his eyebrows.

Miss Pimm understands instantly. 'Ah,' she says. 'Yes,' returning the smile with a little one of her own, and produces the packet of Regal Kingsize, and a box of matches, placing them on the table.

'Thanks,' says Jimmy, and lights a cigarette, sucking deeply.

Jimmy sucked deeply on the joint that Dave passed him. He copied what he had seen Dave and others do: swallowed the smoke and retained it in his lungs for some time before exhaling. He offered the joint back.

'No,' Dave said. 'You'll need another couple of draws for it to have any effect.'

Jimmy took a couple more mouthfuls. They were in the squat, sitting on the mattress. It had been a bad day. By now Jimmy's money had long since been spent, and they had arrived late at the back door of the takeaway, and all the food had gone. Dave had tried to shoplift something to keep them going but he had been followed, he knew, from the moment he entered the supermarket. So, they had gone the whole day without eating. Not for the first time though. Hunger was quite regular, but for some reason that day had been particularly hard.

'All I feel is fuzzy,' Jimmy said.

'Take it easy,' Dave told him. 'You're too tense.'

Jimmy lay back on the mattress and relaxed. Shortly, he felt the fuzziness leave him, and a lovely calm settle within him. The pangs of hunger vanished, and he was sort of drifting.

Dave smiled. 'Good, eh?'

'Not bad,' Jimmy conceded. 'Not bad at all.'

'Just don't get too fond of it, pal. Pass it over.'

Miss Pimm waits until he has smoked almost half the cigarette, fiddling with her papers, pretending to look for some particular statement. Then she purses her lips. She makes a steeple from her fingers and places the point of the spire under her chin. 'I was speaking to your father this morning, Jimmy,' she announces.

Jimmy stares at her.

'He's here in London. With your mother. They'll be coming in to see you this afternoon.'

Jimmy stays quiet.

'He is very, *very* concerned.'

Jimmy blows a long stream of smoke from his mouth. He watches it dissipate, and says, 'I bet.'

Miss Pimm decides it's her turn to say nothing. She watches Jimmy, waiting for him to add something. Then, by way of encouragement, she adds, 'He genuinely is.'

'Oh, sure.'

Miss Pimm doesn't like this attitude. 'I cannot understand, Jimmy—what I mean is—you keep telling me nothing happened at home to *make* you leave—that you just up and left on a whim—and yet you're so—well, so downright antagonistic towards your father.'

Jimmy stubs out the cigarette in the metal ashtray, taking his time about it, mashing it. Then he leans back in his chair, and stares at Miss Pimm, almost insolently.

'It's not normal,' Miss Pimm tells him.

Jimmy bursts out laughing. 'No, it sure ain't *normal*, is it?' he asks through his laughter. 'Well, just maybe I'm *not* normal,' he says, making a ridiculously manic face. 'Maybe I'm really weird,' he adds.

Miss Pimm is not impressed by such antics, but she decides to take his statement seriously. 'No, I don't think you're weird, at all, Jimmy. You are, certainly, very complex. Far more complex than you would like us to think. There's a lot more to you than you're telling us.'

'That's only 'cause you *want* there to be more. Looks good in that—' he jabs a finger at Miss Pimm's folder '—doesn't it? Makes you all look right clever dicks for sorting out all my complexes and all that stupid crap.'

'That's not the case, Jimmy.'

'No?'

Miss Pimm shakes her head, looking quite sad. 'No,' she says firmly, and Dr Rutherford gives a small cough, perhaps in agreement.

Graham coughed an awful lot the night he died, and he was still coughing as life shivered out of him.

'Shit,' Dave said. 'He's dead, I think.'

Jimmy stared down at the body. Although still in his teens, Graham, in death, looked like a wizened old man, but he looked happier than he had for as long as Jimmy had known him.

'We better call someone—the hospital or the police,' Jimmy said vaguely.

'Hell no,' Dave said quickly. 'You and me, we get out of here as fast as fuck.'

'We can't just leave him.'

'Yes, we bloody well can. And we're going to. Don't want to get mixed up with that, pal. He's been pumping heroin into himself for years. We'll be in right shit if we even say we've heard of him.'

'But—'

'Fuck the buts. Get your things and let's get out of here.'

'What things?' Jimmy demanded, suddenly feeling angry.

'Huh? Oh, yeah. I forgot we'd sold them.'

There was a little bit about Graham in the paper a few days later. It just said that the body of a young man found in a squalid, abandoned house had been identified as that of Graham Thompson, 19, and that he had died of an overdose of heroin in the Maryhill area of Glasgow. It mentioned that the squat was used by vagrants.

'Some bloody obituary, eh?' Dave asked.

Jimmy said nothing. For the first time since he had left home he felt scared, really scared. Afraid. Since they had abandoned the squat they had been sleeping in doorways, huddled together, and now both of them were cold and wet and hungry.

'Dave?'

'Hmm?'

'Got any hash?'

'Enough for a joint. Maybe two.'

'Let's get stoned.'

'Not on what I've got.'

'Let's try, anyway.'

'Gettin' to you, is it?'

Jimmy nodded.

'You'll be okay.'

'Yeah.'

'—not trying to trap you,' Miss Pimm is saying. 'Jimmy? Are you listening?'

'What?'

'I said we're not trying to trap you into saying anything. You've admitted the—the killing, and you've been charged. All I'm—we're—Dr Rutherford and I—all we're interested in is to find out what made you—what the circumstances were. We really are trying to help you.'

'Thanks,' Jimmy says wryly.

'Something dreadful must have happened to make you kill that man.'

Jimmy lights another cigarette, holding the match in his fingers, watching it intensely as it burns, only dropping it into the ashtray when the flame touches his flesh. 'It's a long story,' he says at last.

'We're here to listen,' Miss Pimm tells him, leaning forward a little, her eyes brightening.

'Okay,' Jimmy says, trying to blow a smoke ring, but failing.

Miss Pimm blinks, and Dr Rutherford sits up straight, and looks alert for the first time.

Jimmy draws again hard on the cigarette. 'I'll tell you all about it after I've seen my parents—all right?'

Miss Pimm looks disappointed, but tries to hide it behind a tight smile. 'Very well, Jimmy.'

'Unless—' Jimmy begins, and then stops.

'Unless what?' Miss Pimm asks quickly.

Unless Dad admits to Mum that I wasn't lying, Jimmy wants to say, but doesn't. 'Unless nothing,' he says. 'I'll tell you,' he says.

Miss Pimm relaxes. 'Good. You'll see. You'll feel much better when you do—when you get it all off your chest.'

'Yeah.'

'You again?'

''Fraid so.' The constable hands Jimmy the tray with his lunch on it, and adds, 'How's it all going?'

'It's going,' Jimmy tells him, eyeing the piece of battered fish and the soggy chips.

'You'll feel better when you've told them what they want to know.'

Jimmy laughs.

'Did I make a joke?'

'That's what she said—that I'd feel better.'

'She's right.' The constable leaned forward conspiratorially. 'Between you and me I don't have much truck with those psychologists and things. Got more villains off charges than they're worth. But she is right when she says you'll feel better.'

'If you say so.'

'Look, maybe I'm speaking out of turn, but we know you're no villain. Believe me, if we thought you were we wouldn't be wasting our time on you—just bung you off to some remand centre and wash our hands of you.'

'I might be. Could be fooling you.'

'No you're not.' The constable shook his head firmly. 'We've seen plenty of *real* villains in our time—some of them younger than you even—and I can tell you, you're not one of them.'

'I killed him.'

'Yeah, we know that. But there's killing and killing, isn't there? Tell you something else I shouldn't—we know quite a bit about him too.'

Jimmy looked up.

'Oh, sure. He was known to us, don't worry, and we can make a pretty good guess as to what the reason behind your attack was. But

we need you to tell us. Just tell them up there why you killed him—
that's all. You didn't just bump him off for the hell of it the way some
of the young thugs we get in here would.' He gave a wan smile and
shook his head as though even the thought of some of the young thugs
amazed him. 'You wouldn't believe some of the reasons they give for
killing a total stranger—didn't like his face, didn't like the way he
walked, didn't like the way he looked at me, didn't like the colour of
his hair—so they knife some poor sod, or kick him to death. You take
my advice, young man. Tell them everything they want to know, and
it'll be all the better for you when it comes time to go to court.'

'I've said I'd tell them—her—Miss Pimm.'

'You have?' The constable sighs as if that was a great weight off his
shoulders. 'That's good. That's really good.' He goes to the door.
'You know your parents are coming this afternoon?'

Jimmy nods.

'That worry you?'

'Naw.'

'Sure?'

Jimmy smiles. 'I'm sure.'

'That's all right then. Anyway, there'll be someone there with you.'

'Huh?'

'One of us. To keep an eye on things. Probably a WPC—
policewoman.'

'Oh.'

Alone, Jimmy eats his lunch, forcing the food down, and then lies
back on his bunk. He closes his eyes and immediately Dad and Mum
loom into his consciousness, scowling and angry. He snaps his eyes
open again, and stares at the ceiling. When, later, he hears the
footsteps stopping outside his door, he stands up. The key turns and
the door is opened. 'Visit,' a burly sergeant with a moustache tells
him, and Jimmy swings away to the plastic bucket in the corner, and
vomits.

Mum is sitting in a chair, the same kind of chair that he had used in the interview room, but not leaning back, and Dad is standing with his back to the door, his hands clasped behind him, swaying a bit, his head down.

'James—' Mum says, and starts to stand up, but then she sees the policewoman who has followed Jimmy into the room and has taken up her position just inside the door, staring into space and trying to give the impression she's not listening, so Mum stays seated. But she holds out her arms. 'Oh, James,' she says again.

Jimmy ignores the outstretched arms and makes his way to the opposite side of the table, and sits down. Deliberately he turns his head towards the policewoman and asks, 'Any chance of a fag?'

'I don't—' the policewoman begins, and then, with the flicker of a sympathetic smile, 'Hang on.' She opens the door and sticks her head out, calling quietly to someone. When she closes the door again she has a lighted cigarette in her fingers. 'There you go,' she says.

'Ta.'

'Oh, James,' Mum says yet again, only maybe this time she's disapproving of him smoking.

'So, what's all this about, Jimmy?' Dad asks suddenly, spinning round and walking across the room, standing by the table, looking down.

'Been arrested, haven't I?'

'Don't be so flip,' Dad says.

'But you didn't do it, did you, darling?' Mum asks.

'Don't answer that,' Dad interrupts quickly, glaring at the policewoman.

Jimmy gives a short, tired laugh. 'They know I did it, Dad. Caught me red-handed like they say.'

'Oh, James,' seems to be all that Mum can muster, and she starts sobbing, dabbing her eyes with a pretty, lace-trimmed hankie. 'You can't have. You wouldn't do such a thing.'

'Happens all the time,' Jimmy tells her.

'Not killing people,' Mum says, and then frowns as if unsure what she means by that.

'Yes, killing people,' Jimmy says, and looks pointedly at his father. 'You don't have to leave them dead just to kill them, you know,' he says, and then sucks on his cigarette, staring at the smoke as it curls away from him, blinking as some of it enters his eyes and makes them water.

'Oh, James,' says Mum, probably thinking he's crying. Then, as though it has just registered, she asks, 'What did you mean by that—you don't have to leave them dead just to kill them?'

Jimmy blows out a stream of smoke, and through it he says, 'Ask Dad.'

'Cameron—?' Mum asks, turning towards Dad and looking up at him.

But Dad ignores the jibe. Perhaps he doesn't understand it. Perhaps he didn't even hear it. 'They can't *know*,' he tries.

'Of course they know, Dad. They *caught* me there.'

'But you haven't admitted anything, have you?'

'Yes.'

Dad gets annoyed. 'That was a damn stupid thing to do.'

'But you didn't *mean* to do it, did you, dear?' Mum hopes.

Jimmy nods carefully. 'Yes. I meant to do it. I'd do it again if I had to.'

'Oh, my God,' Mum says and starts to sob again.

'You should have denied it,' Dad insists. 'At least until we'd arranged a solicitor for you.'

'I didn't want no fucking solicitor.'

'James!' Mum looks shocked, but it stops her sobbing.

Dad ignores the language. 'You should have denied it and made them prove it. That's what our justice system is all about.'

'Oh, our justice system? Great. Well, I couldn't deny it, could I?' Jimmy says, adding, 'I didn't want to deny it either.'

'And what about us?' Mum asks suddenly.

Jimmy stares at her. 'What about you?'

'The disgrace, James. The disgrace and humiliation you've brought on us. It will quite ruin your father, you know that, I suppose?'

Jimmy puffs out his cheeks and blows hard. 'Yeah, well, maybe it will be good for *him* to be ruined.'

'James!' Mum exclaims.

'It's all right, Alice,' Dad says, beginning to look uneasy. 'Let me handle this, will you please?'

But:

'And this—this psychologist they have questioning you—' Mum puts in.

'How did you know about—?'

'Because they told us, of course. They had to. We're your parents, in case you'd forgotten.'

'Oh, I hadn't forgotten.'

'Alice, please,' Dad says.

'What's she for?' Mum wants to know. 'You're not mad,' she says defiantly as if any implication of madness reflected on her.

'Just asking questions,' Jimmy explains. 'Trying to find out *why* I did it.'

'Oh,' Mum says.

'And why I left home,' Jimmy adds wickedly, staring at Dad and feeling pleasure as Dad reddens and starts to move away from the table.

'Yes. That's another thing,' Mum says sharply. 'Why *did* you leave home, James? It was a cruel thing to do—going off like that without a word, and leaving us to worry ourselves sick.'

'Oh, shit,' Jimmy says quietly.

'That's certainly not an answer, James.'

'Ask him,' Jimmy says, jabbing his cigarette towards Dad.

There is a sudden, frightened stillness in the room. Mum and Dad both try to avoid looking towards the policewoman, but both fail, and their eyes flick towards her and away again several times.

'Not that again, James, please,' Mum says at last.

'Alice,' Dad says in a low, warning voice.

'Yes, Mum. You'd better be careful. We can't have dear old Dad getting into any trouble, can we?'

'Jimmy—' Dad's voice pleads.

Jimmy looks away, looks towards the policewoman, leaving Dad to suffer a bit. Then he looks back to his father, staring him straight in the eyes. 'Don't worry, I haven't said anything,' he says. 'About that,' he adds, lowering his voice.

Dad's shoulders relax, and he reaches out to touch Jimmy, his eyes still pleading.

Jimmy leans away. 'Not yet, I haven't.'

'I should certainly hope not,' Mum snaps.

'Alice—please,' Dad says.

'But Cameron—'

'Just be quiet, dear, will you?'

'Why don't you tell her, Dad?' Jimmy asks reasonably.

Dad swings away, and starts to pace up and down the room, his head bowed. In the corner the policewoman stifles a sneeze, and Dad jumps.

'Bless you,' Jimmy says.

'Thanks,' the policewoman says, and the two of them share a smile that seems to put them on the same side.

'Why are you doing this to us, James?' Mum asks in a loud whisper, breaking the silence half-heartedly.

Jimmy ignores her. 'Tell her, Dad—please,' he says. 'Just tell her.'

'You know we both love you, and yet all you seem determined to do is to destroy—' Mum is saying.

'Dad, please tell her I wasn't lying,' Jimmy begs. 'That's all I want. Just so she knows I wasn't lying.'

Dad stops his pacing. He turns and stares at Jimmy. His eyes are dull and he looks grey and old. 'Jimmy,' he says. 'We do love you, you know.'

'Yes. So you keep telling me. But just tell Mum the truth, will you?'

'This is quite ridiculous,' Mum snaps suddenly, and jumps to her feet, sending the chair scudding away a few feet behind her. She tucks her nice little handbag under her arm in a small defiant gesture. '*I'm* certainly not going to sit here and—'

'Alice—will you please shut up!' Dad shouts.

Mum stands there for a few seconds with her mouth open. She licks her glossy lips. Then she gropes behind her for the chair, finds it and pulls it back towards her. Slowly she sinks onto it, her face drawn. 'So it *is* true,' she says in an appalled whisper.

Dad rounds on her, looking as if he might strike her. Then he turns away and faces Jimmy. He fixes his eyes on Jimmy's face. 'No, it is *not* true,' he says in a cold, clear voice.

For a long time Jimmy stares back, nodding slowly. Then he heaves himself out of his chair and walks towards the door. 'Let me out, will you?' He asks the policewoman.

'Jimmy—' Dad's voice calls behind him.

'Let me out,' Jimmy says again.

'Jimmy—please,' Dad says.
'Just let me fucking out!' Jimmy screams.

Miss Pimm is looking quite upset. She is standing when Jimmy is brought in, and she moves towards him looking, for a moment, as if she is about to cuddle him. But she doesn't: she puts a comforting arm about his shoulder and guides him towards his chair. 'Sit down, Jimmy,' she says quietly, and removes her arm and fetches cigarettes from her bag in a single economical gesture. She waits until Jimmy has lit his cigarette and blown out the match before saying, 'Are you all right?'

Jimmy puffs away on the cigarette, then smiles. 'I'm fine.'

'Really?'

'Really. Hey—I thought we weren't meeting again until tomorrow.'

Miss Pimm nods and goes round the table to her chair. 'It's just that I heard about your visit—that it didn't go too well,' she explains, and sits down.

Jimmy snorts. 'You know what parents are like.'

Miss Pimm prolongs her nod. 'Yes,' she says. 'I know they can be difficult at times.'

'That's one way of putting it.'

Miss Pimm, on impulse, reaches out and takes hold of one of Jimmy's hands. Suddenly embarrassed, Jimmy asks, 'You making a pass at me?'

Miss Pimm smiles sadly. 'Jimmy—look, part of my job is to find out *why* young people do things, but another part, a far more important part is to help them, and to see to it that they don't get punished for things that—well, for things that—Jimmy, what was it you wanted your father to tell the truth about?'

'Huh?'

'I was told you kept begging your father to tell your mother the truth about something.'

'Oh, *that*. It was nothing.'

'I think it was important. I was told you were very upset about it.'

'By that cop?'

'Yes.'

'She got it all wrong.'

'I don't think so.'

'Look, it was nothing. Honest.'

'Well, if it was nothing, why not tell me about it?' She jiggles his hand a little in a friendly, cajoling way. 'I understand you pleaded with your Dad to admit that you hadn't been lying.'

Jimmy makes a dismissive face. 'It was just something that happened.'

'What something?'

Jimmy sighs and manages a grin. 'You're imagining a lot more than what actually happened, you know.'

'Well, if you tell me about it I won't have to imagine, will I?'

'Just Mum thought I stole something that I didn't.'

Miss Pimm looks doubtful. 'That's all?'

'Yep. That's all. I told you it was nothing.'

'Then why did you make such a fuss about it? I mean, why is it so important to you that your father—'

'Look, I told you it was nothing. Just drop it, will you?'

Miss Pimm opens her mouth to respond, but immediately Jimmy continues, 'Can I go now?'

Miss Pimm lets go of his hand, and stands up. 'Very well,' she says. 'You can go. But just you understand that I don't believe what you told me. I don't really believe it was nothing—whatever it was.'

'Please yourself.'

'If your father—'

'Just leave my Dad out of this, will you?'

'If your father was—'

'He's great, my dad. The best dad anyone could wish for. Satisfied?'

'Frankly, no.'

'Well, that's your tough luck.'

'No, Jimmy. It's yours, I'm afraid.'

'Okay. Great. It's mine.'

'Tell you something—when I make my first million I'm going to have to employ you to look after me,' Jimmy says as the constable brings him his tea.

'You'll need a million.'

'I bet.' Jimmy takes the tray and puts it on the bunk beside him. He takes the mug of tea and holds it in both hands as if warming them. 'What did that policewoman have to go and make up stories about me and my dad for anyway?' he asks.

'She didn't make up stories. Just said what she saw and heard.'

'Spying, like.'

'Reporting what she saw and heard.'

'Yeah, well, she heard wrong, and she must need specs.'

'Maybe.'

'No maybe about it. Definitely.'

The constable hesitates for a few moments and then goes to the door, closes it over, and returns to the bunk, standing over Jimmy. 'Mind if I sit?'

Jimmy shrugs and moves up a bit on the bunk. Then he reaches out and takes up the hamburger from the tray and starts to eat deliberately, munching each mouthful only a couple of times before swallowing, staring blankly at the cell floor.

'Now, don't you say anything,' the constable tells him. 'Just listen to me for a bit, will you? It wasn't any accident that that particular WPC was put in there to supervise your visit, lad. There was a damn good reason for that. She's—well, let's just put it this way—she's had special training.'

'Okay, so she's an intellectual—'

'There's some things you can't hide no matter how hard you try.'

'Oh, really. Now that *is* interesting.'

'The WPC saw the way your old man looked at you, and she knows that look. She's seen that look a hundred times. That's what she's been trained to spot. And she's pretty certain she knows now the reason you ran away from home.'

Jimmy keeps on munching, increasing the speed, stuffing more food into his mouth almost before he has swallowed what is already there.

'She *knows*,' the constable tells him quietly. 'And *I* know,' he adds. He gazes up at the ceiling. 'You're not the first kid who's—' He hesitates and changes his gaze to the keys he dangles from one finger. 'We've had kids in here in a worse state than you.'

'Aw,' says Jimmy in mock commiseration.

'He was abusing you, wasn't he?'

Jimmy uses the last piece of crust to wipe sauce from his plate, but he only eats half the crust, using the rest to swab the plate round and round and round.

'You can take it from me that the only way out is to talk about it. Tell someone. Anyone. Just as long as you don't keep it all bottled up inside of you.' The constable stands up and stretches, turning his back on Jimmy. 'And the longer you keep these things to yourself, the harder it gets to let go. You know what happens then? You start blaming yourself, thinking you're the one who's been at fault, and that, pal, is when you blow your mind.'

Jimmy gives him a sly look. 'You seem to know a lot about it.'

The constable doesn't look round. He bends back his head as though easing a crick in his neck. 'I had a mate—'

'Oh, yeah?'

'Blamed himself for twenty years before someone made him see what a bloody moron he was.' He gives a long slow shudder like a horse shaking itself. 'Twenty bloody years,' he repeats, mostly to himself, and sighs. Then he turns, planting a stiff smile on his face. 'Finished?' he asks, and reaches out to take the tray. 'Think about what I've said, will you? If you—if you—if you decide you want to confide in someone, you can use me if you want. Just give us a shout. Constable Hogan. Danny Hogan. I won't—I mean, nothing you say will surprise me.' He walks to the door, backwards. 'Okay?'

Jimmy nods without looking up.

'Like I told you, you're not alone, you know. There's hundreds like you. Thousands, probably, if the truth was known.'

Jimmy puts his head in his hands.

'Don't you forget now. Danny Hogan—if you need me.'

Jimmy doesn't make a move.

'Any time. Even if I'm not on duty someone'll get me,' Constable Hogan tells him, and moves to go.

'That mate of yours—what happened to him?' Jimmy asks suddenly.

The constable shrugs. 'He's making out.'

98

Jimmy nods. 'Good.'

'Yeah.'

'I mean it.'

'I know you do. And don't worry. You'll make out too.'

'Sure I will.'

Constable Hogan stares at Jimmy for a few seconds, and then leaves the cell. He closes the door quietly behind him, and locks it.

It is some time before Jimmy hears his boots padding up the corridor. Hogan seems to be measuring his stride like he was on parade, or at a funeral, or something.

Jimmy lies back on his bunk. In another cell someone lets out a long, low, despairing wail that echoes frighteningly in the silence. Jimmy stares at the light set into the ceiling, not blinking, enjoying the way it blinds him. He wishes there was some such device that would blind his mind.

BOOK THREE

LONDON

VIII

Some tactic has been agreed, clearly. Miss Pimm pointedly avoids any mention of the visit. Indeed, to begin with, she is quite sharp and business-like as if determined not to allow her questioning to be undermined by any sympathy she might feel.

Dr Rutherford is not there. His place has been taken by a policewoman who sits in Dr Rutherford's chair and looks very young. She sits up very straight in the chair, her knees together, her hands folded primly on top of them like a nun. When she notices Jimmy looking at her she seems unsure whether to smile or not: the manual hasn't told her about this. So, she lets a thin smile hover on her lips for a moment, then drops it, then brings it back once more before looking away.

Miss Pimm follows Jimmy's gaze, and says, 'That's WPC Patterson.'

'Oh?'

Miss Pimm offers no explanation as to why WPC Patterson is there. She opens her file, and Jimmy notices a lot of things have been written up, the headings underlined in red, and some crucial phrases overlayed in yellow. 'So,' she says, 'we had reached the point, I think, when you said you were going to tell me about London?' She raises her eyebrows.

'Oh—yeah,' Jimmy says vaguely as if he can only just remember making such a commitment.

'In fact,' Miss Pimm continues, keeping her voice on a nice even keel, and looking carefully at her notes, 'You did say you would tell me everything.'

'Did I?'

'I have it written down.'

'And that means I said it, does it?'

'Yes.'

Jimmy gives a little chuckle.

Miss Pimm keeps her face serious, but she does bring out the matches and cigarettes and slides them across the table.

'That a bribe?' Jimmy asks good-humouredly.

'No. I'll take them back if you like,' Miss Pimm tells him.

'Like hell,' Jimmy says, and grabs the cigarettes, lighting one slowly, squinting as the smoke curls into his eyes.

'And I'm hoping that means you'll tell me why you killed that unfortunate man.'

'Unfortunate? Is that what you think he was?'

Miss Pimm looks interested. 'Wouldn't *you* think so?'

'No, I bloody wouldn't.'

'Indeed? And why not?'

Jimmy just stares at her.

'Nobody deserves to be murdered, Jimmy,' Miss Pimm tells him, but there is something goading about her tone.

'No?'

'No.'

'Not even—' Jimmy begins, and then stops abruptly, a curiously wary look creeping into his eyes. He tries to hide this by blinking rapidly, and waving his hand at the smoke as though blaming it.

'I'm listening,' Miss Pimm encourages quietly.

Jimmy shakes his head. 'Nothing.'

Miss Pimm now closes her eyes too, snapping them closed and open again in her peculiar small way of showing annoyance. 'You keep doing that,' she complains tightly.

'Doing what?'

'Starting to say something and then stopping. It's most irritating.'

Jimmy smiles indulgently. 'Yeah. That's what my mum says.'

—I'm sure he does it purposely just to annoy me, Mum told Dad.

—Why would he do that? Dad asked, not really interested.

Mum said, I don't know.

Dad said, Exactly.

—Always when I'm busy, too. He makes me stop what I'm doing and then leaves me there dangling, Mum complained.

—I'm sure you just imagine it, Alice, Dad said.

'So why do you do it?' Miss Pimm asks.

'Because.'

Miss Pimm tuts. '*That's* not an answer.'

'Because I find it's just not the right time to say it.'

Miss Pimm gives this her serious consideration, and apparently understands what he means. 'I see,' she says.

But Jimmy shakes his head. 'No, you don't.'

'Well, explain it to me then, please.'

'Can't. Even if I tried you still wouldn't really understand.'

'I'm not altogether stupid, Jimmy,' Miss Pimm says, clearly irked, and getting a little flustered.

'I didn't mean it like that,' Jimmy tells her.

They sit there, opposite each other, in silence for some time. Jimmy wins. Miss Pimm blinks suddenly, and looks down at her files. 'Right,' she says finally. 'London. Tell me about that, will you? You promised you would.'

'What d'you want to know?'

'Everything. How did you get down there for a start?'

'Hitched,' Jimmy says curtly.

'We've got to do *something*,' Jimmy said.

'Like what?' Dave asked.

'I dunno. Something. I'm starving again.'

Dave guffawed. 'You're always starving. Never known anyone like you for packing it away.'

'I'm a growing lad,' Jimmy told him with a smile.

It was one of those cold, wet, dreary days that are peculiar to

Glasgow, the wind using the steep streets to gather speed, and whip the rain into a soaking sheet that penetrated everything.

'Okay,' Dave said. 'I'll go and see what I can lift.'

'I'll do it,' Jimmy said suddenly.

'*You'll* do it? Don't be cracked. They'll see you coming a mile off. This takes talent, pal, and talent for lifting you ain't got.'

'If you can do it, I can do it.'

'Oh, yeah? Okay, then. *You* do it.'

'Right.'

They chose a small, Pakistani-run shop, the kind that sold just about everything in small quantities. Dave had lifted from it a few times before and had got away with it, so maybe their luck would hold. 'I'll do the chatting and you get the stuff,' Dave said. 'Just be quick and don't look guilty.'

'What you mean—don't look guilty?'

'Don't try not looking at the Paki. Look him right in the eye when you're coming out. Stop and ask him for something you know he won't have. A metal comb is a good bet. They don't keep them, just plastic ones.'

'Okay.'

But it didn't work out as planned. The owner of the store watched them like a hawk, and no matter how Dave tried to distract him, his eyes followed Jimmy.

Up and down the aisle Jimmy went, waiting for his chance. But no chance came. Dave called, 'Find what you want?'

'No.'

'What you looking for?' the owner asked.

'Metal comb,' Jimmy said.

'No,' the owner said.

'Fuck it, come on,' Dave called. 'Let's go to a *decent* shop.' He went to the door and held it open.

Suddenly, on some crazy impulse, Jimmy grabbed a couple of tins from the shelf, and dived out the door. They raced like mad things down the road, roaring with laughter. They ducked down a narrow alleyway, cutting through into Hope Street. Breathless, they dashed into Ladbrokes, not going into the betting shop itself but staying in the long entry passage.

'What'd you get?' Dave asked.

Jimmy pulled the two tins from under his anorak and handed them over.

Then they were laughing again, hooting until the tears rolled down their faces. 'Fucking lychees and kidney beans,' Dave gasped.

'Main course and pudding,' Jimmy said, and that started them off again.

'All they'll do is give us the shits,' Dave said.

'Got to keep the bowels moving,' Jimmy said.

'Not that frigging much. Hey, mate,' Dave said to a forlorn-looking punter making his way from the shop. 'You want some delicious lychees and beans?' But the man didn't answer. He looked puzzled at first, then frightened, and scuttled away. 'See. Nobody wants the things,' Dave said, grinning hugely. 'Let's dump them.' He tossed the cans into a wastepaper holder. 'Some lifter you turned out to be.'

'The trouble with you is you've no taste,' Jimmy told him, and again they were laughing, walking up Hope Street with something of a swagger.

But the rain driving into their faces and seeping into their clothes soon dampened their spirits. They decided to shelter for a bit in the doorway of a travel agency, stamping their feet to keep them from going numb. And perhaps it was the sheer misery of the day, or perhaps it was the gnawing of hunger, or perhaps it had something to do with the glossy brochures in the window beside them, that made Dave suddenly revive the suggestion, 'What say we piss off to London?'

'Now?' Jimmy asked.

'Now,' Dave said firmly.

'Right now? This minute?'

'Why the hell not?'

'Jeez.'

'Come on. It'll be a right laugh.'

Jimmy took a deep breath. 'Okay,' he said.

'Let's go then.'

They made their way to the underpass, hopping over puddles, jostling each other, play-acting like children. 'Mind you,' Dave admitted as they stood under the sign for Carlisle, thumbs stuck out hopefully, 'It's a lousy day for hitching. No bastard wants two wet scruffy sods like us messing up their nice posh cars.'

'Now you tell me.'

'Well, when you get your BMW are *you* going to let crap like us into it?'

For some mad reason that made them start laughing again, and they were still laughing when the Volvo station-wagon swished to a stop. The driver tooted his horn.

'Come on for shit sake,' Dave yelled.

'I'm coming.'

'How long did that take—to hitch from Glasgow to London?' Miss Pimm wants to know.

Jimmy screws up his face. 'A day, about.'

'That quick?'

Jimmy nods and gives a broad grin.

'You're smiling,' Miss Pimm points out.

'Just thinking of something,' Jimmy tells her. 'Nothing important.'

Dave fastened his seat belt, sitting beside the driver, leaving Jimmy to wedge himself into the back with the pile of what looked like fabric samples. 'Thanks for stopping,' Dave said. 'Nice car.'

I think it's a *very* nice car, Mum said, when Dad drove home in the new Audi, and they all stood round admiring it.

I think so, Dad agreed. What about you, Jimmy?

I've seen it on television, haven't I? Mum interrupted.

I'm sure you have, Alice, Dad said.

It's the one with that German—Mum began.

Vorsprung durch Technik, Jimmy said.

That's the one, Mum said admiringly, giving Jimmy a pride-filled look as if he could now speak German fluently.

You like it, Jimmy? Dad asked again.

Very nice, Dad.

Good. As long as you like it.

Oh, I see. I don't count, Mum said, not angry or anything, but pouting.

'Been standing there long?' the driver asked.

'Too long in this,' Dave said, pointing to the rain banging on the wind-screen. 'Maybe half an hour.'

'Wasn't going to pick you up,' the man confessed. 'Don't usually stop when there's two. Don't like anyone sitting behind me,' he said, peering at Jimmy through the rear-view mirror. 'Friend of mine got mugged that way. First thing he knew the bloke behind him had a knife at his throat.'

'We won't mug you, mister,' Dave assured him. 'Will we, Jimmy?'

'Naw,' Jimmy said.

The man laughed, albeit a bit nervously. 'Where you heading?'

'London.'

'London, eh?'

'Going to stay with my grandparents,' Jimmy lied glibly.

'Oh,' the man said.

Dave smiled. 'His grandad's pretty big in the police,' he said.

'Oh,' the man said again, and seemed a bit uneasy. 'Well, I'm only going about fifty miles down the road.'

'That's okay. Thanks anyway,' Dave told him.

'What you go and tell him that for?' Jimmy demanded as they stood at the exit of the service station, hitching again.

'Didn't you suss him?'

'What you mean—suss him?'

'He was a poof. Kept brushing my leg as he changed gears.'

'Oh.'

Dave laughed. 'You'll learn. Lots of men who pick up hitch-hikers are poofs.'

'Oh.'

'Some of them are okay though. Just didn't like the look of that one. Something creepy about him. You can usually tell . . . And fuck you too!' Dave yelled suddenly at the two teenagers who roared past them in a clapped-out Fiesta, sticking a finger in the air. 'Mate of mine got gang-raped after being picked up.'

'Shit,' Jimmy said.

'Hey, don't worry. I'll look after you. Nobody's going to touch either of us as long as I'm around. Here we go,' he added as a small van slowed down, and stopped.

'We were lucky,' Jimmy tells Miss Pimm. 'Got a ride from some hippies in a van all the way from just outside Hamilton right down here.'

'That *was* lucky.' Miss Pimm agrees cheerily.

Jimmy nods. 'About the only bit of luck we did have.'

'Oh?' says Miss Pimm.

'All down hill from then on.'

Miss Pimm waits.

'Yeah,' Jimmy says.

Something strikes Miss Pimm. 'You keep saying "we", Jimmy. Who was with you?'

'We? Do I? Meant me. I was by myself.'

'Is that the truth?'

''Course it is.'

'All right,' Miss Pimm says doubtfully. 'I won't argue.'

'So, *I* get to London.'

'And then?'

'Look for somewhere to stay, don't I?'

'And do you find somewhere?'

Jimmy nods.

It was a Friday, and London hummed. Although they were both tired from the journey down, Jimmy and Dave could not resist a trip to the West End. Dave, in particular, wanted to see the lights, see Piccadilly, see the theatres, see everything he had only heard or read about. 'Jeez!' he kept exclaiming. 'Look at *that!*'

Someone had told them of a hostel they could stay in, something called Centrepoint, a place in Soho, so they gravitated there but only with a half-hearted intention of finding the hostel. For the moment they were far more interested in soaking up the atmosphere, intrigued by everything, particularly Chinatown which they came upon purely by accident. 'Like *being* in China, isn't it?' Dave asked.

'Dunno, never been to China,' Jimmy quipped.

'You know what I mean.'

'Stinks a bit,' Jimmy pointed out. 'And look at those,' he added, pointing to the carcases of duck hanging in the restaurant windows.

'They must be that stuff—Bombay duck,' Dave suggested.

'That's fish.'

'What is?'

'Bombay duck.'

'You're kidding.'

'No, I'm not.'

They wandered back down Shaftesbury Avenue, stopping to gaze in fascination at the displays in the shops. Not that they were very different from any they had seen in Glasgow, but this was London, and that made them *seem* different. Seem better. And the smell of pizzas coming from the take-aways near Piccadilly Circus was the best smell they'd ever smelled.

'Look at that stuff,' Dave said.

'I'm looking.'

'Just realised I'm bloody starving.'

'Me too.'

'Want some?'

'You got the money?'

'Don't need money, mate,' Dave said.

'You're not going to—'

'Naw. No need for that yet. Watch.'

A short fat man was balancing a slice of sagging pizza in one hand, trying to manoeuvre it into his mouth. He wore glasses, and peered over them, more interested, it seemed, in the passers-by than in eating. Brazenly Dave walked up to him. 'You're not going to eat all that, are you?' he asked.

The man lowered the pizza, and studied Dave, eyeing him up and down slowly. 'You want it?' he asked.

'Wouldn't mind,' Dave said with a huge, charming smile.

The man smiled too, and handed over the pizza.

'Thanks,' Dave said, taking the pizza and trotting back to Jimmy.

'Hey!' the man called.

'Let's shift,' Dave told Jimmy.

'Hey!' the man called again.

'Come *on*,' Dave said.

They scuttled round the corner, and crossed over the road quickly, stopping at the Eros island, and sitting down on the steps. Dave crammed his mouth with pizza, and passed it over.

'How'd you get him to hand it over?' Jimmy asked, chewing away, wiping some dripping cheese from his chin.

'Easy,' Dave said. 'He didn't really want it. Just using it as an excuse to eye people up. It's an old trick. You see them in Central Station in Glasgow. Buy hamburgers they don't want and just stand there looking about.'

Jimmy shook his head.

'Easy touches, the queers,' Dave pointed out.

'Oh,' Jimmy said.

'So, where was it you stayed?' Miss Pimm asks.

'Can't remember the name of the place. Some hostel someone told us about. A place where homeless kids can stay for a night.'

'Centrepoint?' Miss Pimm suggests.

'Yeah. Yeah—I think that's what it was called.'

'This must be it,' Dave said.

Jimmy grimaced. 'Looks really shitty.'

Dave laughed. 'Probably is.'

It was shittier than either of them had expected. The place stank of stale urine and vomit, and with the pungent odour of the disinfectant that had been used to try and remove both those other smells. They were shown downstairs to a large room converted into a dormitory. Lines of beds on either side and a passageway between them. Most of the beds were occupied, youngsters lying on them, or sitting in twos or threes, talking. Here the strongest smell was of dirty feet. But there was, too, a strange smell of fear, a sweaty smell.

They were shown to two adjoining beds near the door, which was a good thing. Dave pulled back the single brown blanket and made as if to get under it. Then he stepped back. 'Shit,' he said. 'I'm not sleeping in that.'

Jimmy peered at the bed. The sheet, a cream coloured thing was stained with what could have been irremovable blood but was pale enough now to have been anything. He swept the blanket back over the sheet, and lay down on top of the bed, folding his arms behind his head. Jimmy followed his example.

'Tell you what, pal,' Dave said, 'We're going to find something better than this shithole.'

'Yeah,' Jimmy said.

'Christ, we were better off in the squat than here.'

'Yeah.'

'What you think? Should we . . . .'
But Jimmy was already asleep.

I don't think he's sleeping, Mum said.
What makes you say that? Dad asked.
Well, he's all black under the eyes, and he keeps yawning.
He's growing, was Dad's explanation.
What's that got—
It's nature, Dad said. When boys start to grow they sleep badly.
Really? Mum asked, sounding surprised. I've never heard that.
Why should you?' Dad asked.
I just thought I would have, Mum said. Ah, well, you learn something every day, she added, and accepted Dad's explanation as usual.

Crichton, would you kindly wake up and pay attention! Mr Corrigan said. These fractions are hard enough to understand when you're awake.
Yes, Mr Corrigan. I am awake.
Well, stay awake then.
Yes, Mr Corrigan.
   And later, after class, Mr Corrigan called him aside and asked, Are you sure you're all right, James?
I'm fine, Mr Corrigan.
Do you want me to have a word with your parents?
Jimmy stiffened. What for?
Mr Corrigan shook his head in a puzzled way. I'm just not happy about you, James. I think there's something bothering you—or something happening that's making you—well, changing you.

Jimmy forced a hard laugh. There's nothing the matter, Mr Corrigan. Really. If there was, I'd tell you.

Would you?

Yes.

Well, just remember you *can* tell me if—

I'll remember, Mr Corrigan, Jimmy interrupted. Can I go now?

Yes. You can go.

And Jimmy felt Mr Corrigan's eyes following him all the way out of the classroom, and spotted him watching from the classroom window as he crossed the school yard on his way home.

I'm not happy with Crichton, Mr Corrigan happened to say to Mrs Clarke as they sipped coffee together between classes.

Now, that's strange, Mrs Clarke said. I was having—am having the same worries.

I thought it might be bullying but he assures me it isn't.

What about the family?

Fine, as far as I know.

Should we—

Mr Corrigan frowned. Not yet. I mean—it is *Doctor* Crichton we're talking about.

Ye-es. Yes, it is, isn't it?

And they left it there, sipping their coffee still, because doctors were revered people, and powerful people, who could cause quite a bit of trouble if upset.

'We only stayed there the one night, though,' Jimmy volunteers.

'Oh? And why was that?' Miss Pimm asks.

'Ever been in one of those hostels?'

Miss Pimm shakes her head.

'You should try one. They stink. And you can't sleep anyway. Always kids fighting or screaming in their sleep. Like a nut-house.'

'But they're better than nothing, aren't they?'

'No. Better sleeping outside, rough, than in one of those crap places,' Jimmy says.

'Is that what *you* did then? Sleep rough?'

Jimmy nods.

'Where?'

'Huh?'

'Where? Anywhere in particular?'

'No. Just wherever I fancied,' Jimmy says, and appears to be thinking of something else. 'You any idea how *many* homeless people there are here in London?' Jimmy asks after a while.

'Quite a few,' Miss Pimm acknowledges.

'Seems like millions. They're everywhere.'

'Yes. I've seen them,' Miss Pimm says, making her voice appropriately sorrowful.

'The ones you see aren't the half of it,' Jimmy tells her. 'Bet you mean the ones in the Strand and places like that.'

'Well, yes—'

Jimmy gives a tired laugh. 'They're nothing,' he says. They're the ones who *want* to be seen. Kind of fancy themselves for being homeless. The *real* homeless you don't see. They're *ashamed* of being without a home. They hide themselves. Hundreds—thousands of them. From everywhere. All over England, and Scotland, Wales and Ireland. Loads of Irish.'

'Shit,' Dave said. 'We'll never get in there,' he added, leaning sideways and eyeing the length of the queue.

But they did get in, eventually. Several hours later. And after waiting another hour they got to the counter and waited for the black lady to finish what she was doing. Finally, she looked up, raising her eyebrows by way of asking what they wanted. Dave did the talking. 'We need a crisis loan,' he told her.

'Filled in the form?' the lady asked.

'What form?'

The lady made an irritated grimace, and took a form from the shelf beside her. Then she spotted Jimmy. 'Want one for him too?'

'Course I do.'

The lady took another form and handed both over. 'Fill those in and come back when you've done it.'

They took the forms and retreated to one corner of the office. Laboriously they filled in the forms, Dave being oddly secretive about his. Then they queued again, shuffling towards the counter inch by inch. When they got there Dave handed over the forms. 'There you go,' he said, attempting to be cheerful.

Without looking at the forms the lady said, 'Identification?'

'What?'

'Identification. Got to have some identification. You could be anyone.'

Jimmy fumbled in the pocket of his anorak, looking for his passport. His fingers had just found it when Dave kicked him. 'Ain't got none, have we?' Dave told the lady.

'Well you'll just have to go and get some.'

'Like what?'

'Anything that tells me you are who you say you are.'

'Of course we're who we say we are.'

'I need proof,' the lady said adamantly.

'Oh, fuck this,' Dave said. 'Come on, pal.'

'Hang on,' Jimmy hissed. 'Look, miss, it's a *crisis* loan we need. It's a crisis. We're really starving.'

But the woman had clearly heard all this before, and had become immune to tales of starvation. 'Everyone in this room is starving,' she said.

'I bet you're fucking not,' Dave told her.

The woman didn't like that at all. 'I've told you—bring in some identification and we'll see if we can help,' she said. 'Next,' she called, bending, and looking round Dave.

'That was a great idea,' Jimmy told Dave.

'Bastards,' Dave said.

'Why wouldn't you let me show them my ID. I had my passport.'

"Cause. Like I told you. Never tell no one your real name. That's yours, pal. Tell that lot and before you know it you're on every goddamn computer in the country.'

'So what?'

'So what? I'll tell you what. Never escape from it, that's what. Just when you don't expect it—don't bloody want it either—some shithead presses a button and they know all about you. Bugger that for a lark. Tell no one nothing—that's what I say.'

They stood in the doorway of the building, looking about them, watching other people push past them as they made their way in to try and get some support.

'Bastards,' Dave said again.

'Who?'

'Them up there.'

Jimmy giggled. 'You didn't expect them to give us anything anyway, did you?'

Dave took to giggling too. 'No. But it was worth a try.' They wandered away from the building. 'Shit, I'm bloody starving.'

'Me too.'

'We'll have to do something.'

'Yeah. What?'

'I'll think of something.'

'There's always the Sally Army hand-outs,' Jimmy said.

'Fuck that,' Dave said. 'That'd mean going to Wino Land, and we sure as hell ain't going down there. Get your bloody throat cut for a cup of watery soup. No bloody fear.'

Jimmy shrugged.

'Tell you what—let's go down to the river.'

There was something about standing close to the grey, murky Thames that pleased them. Something about the way the seagulls screeched and the barges, tied together, sobbed and heaved like floundered whales, the heavy tarpaulins slung over them hiding unimaginable cargoes. Dave stood on one now, roaring, 'Shiver me bloody timbers!'

'Aye, aye, Mr Christian,' Jimmy said.

'You a Christian?' Dave asked suddenly.

'Used to go to church, if that's what you mean,' Jimmy told him.

'Yeah,' Dave said. 'I suppose that's what I mean.' He waved his arms like a windmill, gazing skyward. 'Wonder if there *is* something up there. You believe that crap about heaven?'

Jimmy shrugged.

Dave jumped down from the barge and with the jump seemed to wipe all thought of paradise from his mind. He squatted, folding his arms across his knees, staring out at the water. 'Tell you something. Some day I'm going to write me this book,' he said.

'Oh yeah?'

Dave nodded firmly. 'Yep. About us.'

'It'll never sell,' Jimmy told him.

'And I'm going to call it *Behind Glass*.'

'Great title,' Jimmy said wryly.

'Know why?'

'Go on, tell me.'

'Because everything we need and want is behind glass,' Dave said seriously. 'Ever thought about that?' He picked up a stone and tossed it into the water. 'Every damn thing. Like today—that old bag stuck behind her protective glass screen. And banks are all glass now. And the things in shop windows. And then you go into a caff and all the food is in glass cases.' Dave tossed another stone, trying to scud this one across the top of the water. 'Know the worst thing of all? Looking into people's windows and seeing them sitting there all warm and cosy with their cups of tea and their telly and us outside freezing our balls off. That's a real bitch.'

'So when you going to start writing?'

Dave looked up with a huge grin. 'Got to learn how to write first, don't I?'

'You can't write?'

Dave shook his head. 'Naw. Can read a bit though.'

'How did you fill in that form back there?'

Dave hooted. 'Didn't, did I? Just put a load of wavy lines and a few squiggles. Let those buggers sort it out.'

'You're something else.'

'What'd I ever need to write for? Never had a job that needed it. Only done a bit of bricklaying. Don't have to write for that.'

'What happens when you make the big time?'

'Get me a secretary, won't I. A big, plump, fabulous blonde. Come on,' Dave said, standing up and wiping his hands across the seat of his jeans. 'Let's go see what we can scavenge.'

Jimmy stood up and wiped his hands on his jeans. Then, suddenly, he said, 'Hang on a tick.' He reached inside his anorak and pulled out his passport. He opened it and gazed for a few moments at the photograph, frowning, as though trying to identify the likeness. Then he snapped it shut and flung the passport into the river.

'What you do that for?' Dave asked.

'Like you said, don't let anyone know who I am.'

Dave grinned. 'Right,' and slapped Jimmy on the shoulder.

Together they watched the passport float down the river.

'Well,' Jimmy said, 'that's me gone.'

'Naw,' Dave told him, 'you can be anyone you want now.'

Jimmy thought about that. 'Yeah, I can, can't I?'

'And what did you live on?' Miss Pimm asks.

'We usually dined at the Ritz,' Jimmy tells her, and Miss Pimm gives him a condescending little titter. 'There's loads of food round if you look for it. Got to get there first though. There's an awful lot of greedy bastards, you know,' he adds with a grin.

'Meaning?'

'Soho's best. All those posh restaurants. They throw out enough food to feed an army,' Jimmy says. 'Or all those Ethiopians,' he adds quietly.

'Oh,' says Miss Pimm with a small wriggle of her nose.

'Nothing wrong with it. It's a bit messed about and cold, sure, but it tastes pretty okay. Anyway, if you gulp it down quick you don't even taste it. Maybe we—I had some of your left-overs, Miss Pimm.'

'I doubt that, Jimmy. I can't afford Soho prices on what I earn.'

'Should put in for a raise.'

But that meant they couldn't settle down to sleep anywhere until well after the restaurants had closed—two, maybe three o'clock in the morning. And that was risky. The police vans patrolled Soho in the early hours, looking for runaways, and drug-pushers, and perverts looking for young boys. And if they caught you, they'd lift you, and you could be charged with anything, even some burglary they wanted to close the file on. But, when a good meal was uncovered, it was worth it.

'Feeding time again,' Constable Danny Hogan says, handing over the tray with a friendly enough grin.

Jimmy stares at the food. 'Had better than this out of a rubbish bin,' he says.

'But not the service with a smile,' Constable Hogan says. 'How's it going upstairs?'

Jimmy shrugs. 'Okay, I guess.'

'Good.'

Jimmy shoves a spoonful of mince and mashed potato into his mouth, and swallows.

'Your dad's been asking to see you again,' Constable Hogan tells him.

'I bet he has.'

'You want to see him?'

Jimmy continues to eat for several minutes, thinking. 'You be there this time?'

'If you want.'

Jimmy nods. 'Okay, I'll see him if you're there.'

'You know I'll be listening?'

'Yeah.'

'And that—'

'And that you'll tell the shrink what you hear—yeah, I know.'

'As long as you know.'

Jimmy shoves some food about his plate, and then he looks up. 'What'd you mean when you said your mate had been there?'

'Been through it.'

'Through what?'

'What I think you've been through.'

Jimmy thinks about that for a while. 'He—him, your mate—he run away?'

'No.'

'Why not?'

Constable Hogan shrugs. 'Too scared, I guess. Things were a bit different when he was your age.'

'Oh,' Jimmy says, and goes back to eating. Then he looks up. 'Yeah, well like I said, I'll see Dad if you're there.'

'Right,' Constable Hogan says, but still waits.

'Yes?' Jimmy asks.

'Just thought you might want to say something more.'

Jimmy shakes his head. 'No.'

IX

'Made it to the Poppy, then?'

'Huh?'

Killing time before a nightly scavenge, Jimmy and Dave sat on the steps surrounding the Eros statue in the centre of Piccadilly Circus. It was early December, the Christmas lights were ablaze in Regent Street, and the shop windows were decorated enticingly. There was no frost, but it was cold enough.

'Made it to the Poppy, I said,' the man repeated, sitting down beside them. He was a little older than either of them, early twenties, but trendily dressed in a Reebok track-suit and flashy trainers.

'What you mean?'

'The Poppy. That's what we call it. This. Eros. The Poppy.'

'Oh,' Dave said. And then, 'Why?'

The young man grinned. 'Because,' he said, lowering his voice significantly. 'Because here's where you get what the poppy gives you. And other things.'

'Oh,' Dave said again.

'Want some?'

'No money.'

'Take a bit anyway. Call it an early Christmas present.' The young man offered a morsel of hash wrapped in clingfilm. 'Go on. Have it.'

Dave took the hash.

'That your mate?' the young man asked.

'Who, him? Yeah.'

'Doesn't say much, does he?'

'Uh-huh. Strong silent type, he is.'

The man nodded. 'Got tobacco?'

Dave shook his head.

'Skins?'

'No.'

'Lucky I came along then. What they call you?'

'Dave.'

'And him?'

'Jimmy.'

'I'm Colin.' He pulled a tin of tobacco from his pocket, opened it and passed over cigarette papers and some tobacco. 'Been here long?'

'Long enough. Too bloody long.'

'Like that, eh?'

'Just like that.'

'Got a place to stay?'

'Yeah,' Jimmy interrupted.

'Oh,' Colin said, sounding a bit disappointed.

'Only a squat,' Dave told him.

'A good one though,' Jimmy said, nudging Dave.

Colin spotted the nudge. 'Hey, come on. I'm not after anything. You got somewhere to stay or not?'

'Yeah, we've got this squat. We told you,' Dave insisted.

'Okay. Okay. How's about money?'

'You handing that out too?'

Colin laughed. 'Am I shit. Hard enough making it for myself. Could put you on to a good thing or two though—if you're interested.'

'Meaning?'

'Well, you know. . . .' He looked about him. 'Like that,' he said, nodding his head towards two men, one sitting, one standing, pretending to talk but sizing up the youngsters sitting about.

'We're not into that sort of shit,' Dave said.

'Just a suggestion. Easy money. Christmas coming up and all.'

'Tell him to piss off,' Jimmy whispered.

'Easily make fifty, sixty quid a night, you two would. Each, I mean.'

Dave rolled a joint, lit it, and drew heavily on it before passing it to Jimmy.

'Free drinks, something to eat and a place to sleep,' Colin went on.

'You some sort of pimp or something?' Dave demanded.

'I got clients. That's all. If I get them the right boy they slip me a few quid. Don't take anything off you.'

'Fucking right you don't. Sooner starve we would, than get into that. Right, eh, Jimmy?'

Jimmy nodded.

'Just trying to help,' Colin said matter-of-factly, and stood up. 'Well, got to go skating. See who wants what. See you.'

'Yeah. See you.'

'And if you change your minds—'

'We won't.'

'We'll see.'

'Wasting your time on us, pal.'

'We'll see. Anyway, I'm around here most evenings.'

Dad is sitting by the table in the visitors' room when Jimmy is brought in. He looks hard at the policeman and asks, 'Can't I speak to my son alone, officer?'

Constable Hogan shakes his head. ''Fraid not, sir.'

'But—'

''Fraid not, sir,' Constable Hogan repeats firmly.

'How are you, Jimmy?' Dad begins.

'Fine.'

'You're not being—being—'

'Molested?' Jimmy asks. 'No.'

Dad winces. 'I meant—'

'I know what you meant, Dad.'

Dad stands up suddenly and walks about the room. Then he rounds on Constable Hogan and says, 'I can't talk to my son with you standing there listening to every word.'

'That's the rule, sir.'

'I don't mind him being there, Dad,' Jimmy says.

'Well I do, dammit.'

'Nothing I can do about that, sir.'

'Well, maybe I can. Who's your superior?' Dad demands, getting really annoyed.

'There's Chief Inspector Harrington, sir.'

'Tell him I want to see him. Instantly.'

'Can't do that, sir. Can't leave you and Mr Crichton alone.'

'But I'm his father,' Dad shouts.

'Yes, sir.'

'This is ridiculous.'

'I can take the prisoner back to his cell and *then* see if the chief inspector can see you.'

'Well, *do* that. I'm sorry, Jimmy. I mean—'

But Jimmy is already on his feet making his way to the door.

There is quite a conference outside the interview room before Miss Pimm bustles in. Jimmy can see the shapes through the glass panel in the door. There are four of them, Miss Pimm and Constable Hogan are two, the other two he doesn't recognise. They keep their voices low, and nod to each other quite a lot. Even through the glass Jimmy can detect an urgency about their conversation, and wonders what they are up to now. He is still wondering when Miss Pimm bustles in. 'I'm sorry to keep you, Jimmy,' she says.

'I've plenty of time,' Jimmy tells her. 'Hogan tell you everything?' he asks mischievously.

Miss Pimm reddens a little. 'He told me what happened earlier. Yes.'

Jimmy nods.

'Your father won't be allowed to see you alone for the time being.'

Jimmy shrugs.

'You don't mind?'

'Would it matter if I did?'

'Well, no.'

'So why ask me?'

'Because it's—it's you—you and your feelings that are important,' Miss Pimm tells him.

'Wow,' says Jimmy.

'Don't you believe that?'

'Yeah, yeah I believe you mean it.'

'Good.'

'What does Dad say?'

Miss Pimm frowns. 'He isn't too happy about it.'

Jimmy smiles. 'I bet he isn't. Used to getting his own way, is my dad.'

Miss Pimm nods.

'What about Mum?'

'What about your mother, Jimmy?'

'Can I see her alone?'

'You want to?'

Jimmy thinks about this. He wants to and he doesn't want to. He knows any visit with Mum will end in a row. She'll always take Dad's side. She won't even try and see his. But . . . 'Yeah, I wouldn't mind.'

'I'll see if I can arrange it then.'

'Thanks.'

'I'm just wondering—' Miss Pimm begins, pausing as if to give herself a little more wondering time, then continuing, 'I'm just wondering, though, if such a visit wouldn't upset you.'

'Sure it will. Upset me like hell, probably. But I'd like to see her again. Just once more,' Jimmy says.

'I'll try and fix it for tomorrow.'

'Thanks.'

'Meanwhile,' Miss Pimm says with a smile, spreading her hands.

'Yeah. I know. What else did I do in London—right?'

'Right.'

Jimmy shook his head. 'You know, it's really hard to tell you.'

'Why?' Miss Pimm sounds concerned, wondering if perhaps she had heard, 'It's really hard to tell *you*.'

'Because I really didn't do anything,' Jimmy says, and Miss Pimm relaxes with a grateful smile. 'You must have done something,' she urges.

Jimmy shakes his head. 'There's nothing *to* do,' he tells her. 'Not when you've no money. All you do is wander about. Looking.' He gives a short snort. 'Looking at nothing.'

'What about a job, Jimmy? Didn't you try and get a job of *some* sort just to tide you over?'

'Sure I tried.' He grins at her good-naturedly. 'When was the last time you looked for a job, Miss Pimm?'

Miss Pimm simpers.

'That's what I thought. There aren't any jobs in London. Not for the likes of me, anyway.'

'What do you mean by that, Jimmy?—not for the likes of me?'

'You know—homeless—no fixed abode or whatever they say. And no experience. They're very big on experience when they don't want you bothering them.'

'Surely you could have found *something*?'

Jimmy shakes his head. 'Nothing.'

'You really did try?'

'Yep.'

'Not even washing dishes?'

'Why "even"?' Jimmy asks. 'That's a prime job, washing dishes is.'

'Oh.'

'Well, I've made up our minds,' Dave announced, rubbing his eyes with his fists and pushing the hair back out of his eyes. 'Today we're going to start looking for work.'

And they did. They began by sprucing themselves up in a public lavatory, flattening their hair and trying to straighten their clothes. And for the next two weeks they faithfully followed a routine, plodding from Job Centre to Job Centre, reading the cards and trying to make applications. But always they came up against the same question: Experience? It applied, it seemed, even for the most menial work.

Then someone told them they were wasting their time, told them the only way to find a job was to go direct, go straight to some restaurant or café and ask the boss if they could wash up for him and carry out the rubbish. That's the only sort of job you'll get, they were told. The sort even the Pakis wouldn't do. So they tried that. 'What we'll do,' Dave said, 'is try and get a job in one of those good places in Soho. That way we can take what we want to eat *before* we put out the rubbish.' He beamed at his cleverness.

But that didn't work either. There always seemed to be someone there before them no matter what time they arrived, or so they were told. Once it looked as though Dave had landed a job, nothing much, just helping to clear out a pub cellar that had been flooded by a burst pipe. But he didn't get it in the end because he made the mistake of admitting he was homeless.

'Oooh, no,' the man said. 'Not if you're on the streets,' he added, and shut the door without any further explanation.

Dave started banging on the door with his fists, but it didn't open. 'Fuck you,' Dave shouted.

'Yeah, and fuck you too,' the man called from inside.

'Nobody wants to know you when you're homeless,' Jimmy tells Miss Pimm. 'They think there's something wrong with you.'

Miss Pimm nods, and seems to understand.

'Anyway, after a couple of weeks I stopped looking.'

'And just wandered about doing nothing,' Miss Pimm says.

'That's right.'

'I'm knackered,' Jimmy said.

'Me too,' Dave agreed.

'And I'm cold.'

'Me too.'

'And hungry.'

'Me too.'

They managed to laugh aloud at their misery. It was raining, a thin sheet of consistent drizzle that soaked you without your noticing it.

'We're two little lambs who have lost our way,' Jimmy intoned.

'Baa, fucking baa, fucking baa,' Dave chorused.

'What are we going to do, Dave?' Jimmy asked later, seriously.

'I'll think of something.'

'Before we die from exposure?'

'Probably.'

'Oh, good.'

It was Sunday morning, and the police had been thick on the ground in Soho the night before, so hunting for food had been abandoned. They had stolen a bottle of milk from outside a house, one that had been there a couple of days, and shared it. That was all they'd had since Friday. Dave had even asked Jimmy if he wanted to go back to Scotland, and Jimmy had considered it but finally said no. '*You* could go home,' Dave had said.

'No. No, I couldn't.'

And Dave had accepted that.

'We could always go sit in a church.'

'What?'

'Be warm,' Dave pointed out. 'Might be something in the poor box too,' he added.

'You can't nick from a church,' Jimmy said.

'Why not? It's for the poor. You don't get any poorer than us two wee laddies.'

'Not from a church.'

''Fraid Baby Jesus might strike you down?'

Jimmy said nothing.

'Well, we can't just keeping walking in this rain. You suggest something.'

Jimmy had nothing to suggest.

'Hang on,' Dave said suddenly, and scooted across the road. Jimmy watched him as he stopped a man and bummed two cigarettes off him. Then he saw the man put his hand in his pocket and pass something over. Dave trotted back. 'Two fags and enough for a bag of chips,' he said triumphantly.

'Thought you said you'd never beg.'

Dave looked hurt. 'That wasn't begging,' he said. 'That was *asking*. Begging's when you sit down in some lousy doorway and stick your paw out. *That's* begging.'

'Oh. Now I know,' Jimmy said.

'All we have to do is find a chippie.'

It took them over an hour to find a chip-shop open. It would have been nice to eat the chips in the shop, but it would have cost them more that way: taking them out knocked a few pence off the price. So they wandered through the drizzle, munching the chips, and passing one of the cigarettes between them, keeping the other for later. 'For when we're really gasping,' Dave said.

Mum gasps.

Miss Pimm had arranged the visit, and Mum had come by herself. She had received permission to see Jimmy alone, and now they sat facing each other across the table. Mum had just told Jimmy that the police had spoken to Dad and hinted they might want to question him, and Jimmy had said, 'I thought they might.' That was when Mum gasped.

'Why would you think that?' she asks sharply.

Jimmy shrugs.

Mum gets very agitated. 'What have you been telling them, James?' she demands.

'Nothing.'

'You haven't been telling those lies—'

'I haven't said anything, Mum,' Jimmy says. 'And they weren't lies.'

Mum dismisses that with a sort of 'pshaw' sound, and a wave of her hand. 'Why are you doing this to us, James? That's what I can't understand. All we've ever done is—'

'Mum—please, Mum. They weren't lies. Dad did—he did what I said. Honestly. But I haven't told anyone.'

Mum blocks that one out. 'And then to kill someone—I mean—what has got into you, James?'

Jimmy sighs. 'It's a long story.'

'Well, I haven't time for any long stories, James. I just do not understand you at all. I don't even *know* you.'

'Look—'

'And what's more, I don't want to know you. You've killed me too, James Crichton. Killed me and ruined your father, dragging him down here and having him questioned by police—by police—we've never had anything to do with the police. I never want to speak to you again, James.'

Jimmy stands up and carefully pushes his chair into the table. He rests his hands on the back of it and, leaning forward, he says, 'You never did speak to me, Mum.'

'Yes I—'

'You spoke at me. You spoke for me. You never spoke *to* me. And when I tried to speak to you you never listened.' Jimmy walks towards the door. 'Or you just said I was lying.' He bangs on the door. 'So it doesn't make much difference if you never speak to me again, does it?' he asks.

And when the door opens he walks away without looking back.

'Was your visit with your mother all right?' Miss Pimm asks, not nosily but in a general way.

'Terrific.'

'Oh. What went wrong?'

'Nothing. Just Mum. She's all upset.'

'That's understandable, isn't it?'

'Oh, sure.'

'Any mother would be, I think.'

Suddenly Jimmy throws back his head and gives a strange howling laugh. 'She's not upset about *me*,' he says bitterly. 'She's upset about what—about what I've done—about how that will affect *her*.'

'Well—'

'You know what she said? She said I'd killed her too. She said I'd ruined Dad. She doesn't give a toss about what he did to—' Jimmy stops suddenly, eyes Miss Pimm nervously, then looks away. 'Anyway,' he adds. 'I really don't care.'

Miss Pimm takes off her spectacles, folds them, and places them on the table. She rubs her eyes with the tips of her fingers, then folds her hands. 'Jimmy,' she asks quietly, 'Did your father abuse you?'

'I love my dad.'

'I know you do. But that's not what I asked.'

'He's great. Gets me everything I want.'

Miss Pimm waits.

'Got me a computer. Took me on trips with him. Even here. Took me to London with him once.'

Still Miss Pimm waits.

'And he loves me. He told me that. Lots of times.'

Miss Pimm sighs but stays silent.

'Always took my side when Mum was getting at me,' Jimmy says.

'Did he abuse you, Jimmy?' Miss Pimm asks again.

Jimmy keeps his head bent, staring at his fingers as he twists them into shapes, crossing them over one another.

'Did you hear me, Jimmy?'

'I heard you.'

'Well, did he?'

Slowly Jimmy shakes his head. Then, suddenly, he starts to cry, great shuddering sobs, and Miss Pimm comes round the table and puts her arm about his shoulder. 'Jimmy, Jimmy, Jimmy,' she says. 'There's nothing for you to be ashamed of if your father *did* do something to you. It can't have been your fault. You can't defend him and keep it all bottled up inside you. You'll ruin your whole life if you do that.'

Jimmy gives a small laugh. 'Some life I've got ahead of me,' he says, wiping his eyes with his fists, and sniffing.

'Here,' Miss Pimm says, and gives him her hankie which she pulls

from her sleeve like a magician. Jimmy blows his nose and crumples
the hankie into a ball. 'Keep it,' Miss Pimm says, and goes back to
her chair.

'Can we leave this?' Jimmy asks.

'If you want, but—'

'Yeah, I want.'

'All right, Jimmy.'

Jimmy stands up. 'Mum says the police are going to question Dad?'

'They might,' Miss Pimm says.

Jimmy nods.

'Does that—does it worry you?'

Jimmy shakes his head. 'No,' he says in a whisper.

'Good. Because it shouldn't.'

'It doesn't.'

'Good.' Miss Pimm goes to the door and has a word with the
policeman outside. 'I'll speak to you later, Jimmy,' she says. 'They'll
give you a cup of tea now, and in about an hour we'll talk again. All
right?'

Jimmy nods.

'Just drink your tea and relax.'

Jimmy nods again.

'See he gets the tea, will you, Sergeant?'

'Yes, ma'am. Come on, lad.'

'Jimmy,' Miss Pimm calls.

Jimmy turns.

'I'm sorry. Nothing.'

Jimmy gives a tired grin. 'You shouldn't do that you know—start
something and then say nothing,' he tells her.

Miss Pimm sends him a sad smile. 'Yes, I know. Speak to you again
in a while.'

'Yeah.'

X

They were back on the steps below the statue of Eros. Back at the Poppy, as Dave insisted on saying. 'Got to get into the swing of things, man,' he said in an exaggerated hippie accent. Then, 'Will we light it?'

'Yeah. Go on. Be a devil.'

They had saved their one remaining cigarette all day, talking themselves out of lighting every time the urge came upon them. But now Dave lit it, bumming a light from a young girl who sat nearby. 'She fancies you, pal,' Dave told Jimmy as he passed over the cigarette. 'Can't keep her wee eyes off of you.'

'Don't be stupid.'

'Look for yourself.'

Jimmy leaned forward and looked round Dave. The girl smiled at him, and Jimmy ducked back.

'What'd I tell you!'

'Not my type,' Jimmy said, suddenly embarrassed.

'Ever made it?' Dave asked.

'Sure. Loads of times.'

'Liar.'

'You?'

Dave nodded. 'Nothing like what it's cracked up to be.' He gave Jimmy a sideways glance. 'You want to try her?'

Jimmy shook his head. 'Naw.'

'Okay,' said Dave, and he seemed pleased. 'Let's skate.'

'You and your skating,' Jimmy scoffed.

'Got to get—'

'Yeah, I know, into the swing of things. Come on.'

They darted across the street, dodging the traffic, and skidded to a stop outside the Body Shop. 'Where you want to go?' Dave asked.

'Dunno.'

'You're the one who wanted to move.'

'I know. Let's go down and see if there's any buskers.'

They wandered off towards Leicester Square, getting the last few drags out of the cigarette as they went. It had stopped raining, but had turned bitterly cold, and when the cigarette was finished they both dug their hands deep into their pockets and hunched their shoulders against the wind.

There were only two buskers, a couple of West Indians singing reggae to a tape on a battered machine. Nobody seemed to be listening to them. Everyone was in a hurry. Everyone going somewhere. Everyone with somewhere to go. Except them.

'Jeez, I'm frozen,' Dave said, hopping from foot to foot and swinging his arms. A couple of skinheads going past jeered at him.

'Ignore them,' Jimmy said, and was pleased when Dave did.

'Bastards,' Dave said under his breath. 'Come on. Let's find somewhere with a bit of warmth.'

They made their way back to Piccadilly, and stood in the doorway of Boots. Pity it was closed. When it was open for business the hot air ducts just inside the entrance provided a wonderful warmth. A lot of cold people gathered there, sauntering off a little way when the security guard came towards them, but returning for another few minutes of comfort when he set off on a tour of the shop.

They hadn't been there long when Dave spotted Colin come up out of the tube station. He wore clean jeans and a smart leather jacket. 'There's that Colin,' he said to Jimmy. 'Maybe I could touch him for a few quid,' and was moving off almost before he had finished speaking.

Jimmy watched. He saw Colin greet Dave with a wide smile, saw him bend his head to listen, saw him place a comforting hand on

Dave's arm. They talked earnestly for several minutes, and then Colin took some money from his pocket and handed it over, making little of his generosity with a small dismissive gesture. Then they talked again, or rather Colin spoke and Dave listened. At one point they both looked across at Jimmy, and Colin gave him a wave, but they looked away again quickly and went back to talking. When they parted Colin gave Dave a friendly pat on the back, waved to Jimmy again, and, oddly, went back down into the tube station.

There was something a bit strange about Dave when he joined Jimmy. He seemed to be thinking about something, worrying about it. 'What's up?' Jimmy asked.

'Huh?'

'What's up?'

Dave brightened. 'Nothing. Got a tenner from him.'

'Oh, yeah?'

'Yep.'

'Just handed you a tenner?'

Dave showed him the ten-pound note.

'Just like that? What you got to do for that?'

For the first time since they'd met Dave got annoyed. 'What you mean by that?'

'Nobody hands over a tenner unless they want something.'

Dave lost his anger and smiled boyishly. 'Well, just wants me to do a little job for him.'

'Oh, yeah? What?'

'Tell you that later. Listen, I've got to get off for a while. Only for a couple of hours. You take this,' Dave said, pushing the tenner into the pocket of Jimmy's anorak. 'Go have something to eat. Meet me here again at—what time is it now?' he asked, glancing round, spotting a well-dressed elderly man passing and called, 'Got the time, mate?'

The man paused, studied Dave, then told him the time. He looked as if he was going to say something else but changed his mind and went on his way. 'Quarter to eight,' Dave said. 'Meet me here again at ten, will you?'

'Where you going?' Jimmy asked.

'I'll tell you all about it later. Just be here at ten. And have something decent to eat. Don't gulp it, pal. Stay in the warm as long as you can.' Then he was gone, glancing for traffic as he raced across the road and disappeared down the tube station.

'You just manage,' Jimmy tells Miss Pimm after she has asked him, 'But how on earth did you manage?'

Miss Pimm smiles. 'I'm not sure I like the sound of that.'

Jimmy smiles back.

'Did you—'

'Yep,' Jimmy admits. 'Now and again. Just for something to eat. The big supermarkets won't go broke on what I nicked.'

'Did you never feel like going home?'

'Sometimes.'

'Why didn't you?'

Jimmy looks away.

Miss Pimm sighs. 'All right, Jimmy. I won't pursue that,' she says tolerantly. She gathers up her papers. 'Now, you have to appear in court tomorrow, you know that?'

Jimmy nods. 'They told me.'

'Then you'll be put on remand.'

Jimmy nods again. 'They told me that too.'

'You'll be moved from here—did they tell you that?'

'Yes.'

'So really, you and I only have today to finish our talk.'

Jimmy nods.

'I need to know as much as possible so I can put a report in. That goes to the court too so they can assess you.'

Jimmy keeps on nodding.

'I'm going to have to ask you about the actual killing,' Miss Pimm tells him. 'Can we deal with that after lunch?'

'There's not much to tell,' Jimmy says quietly.

'Let me be the judge of that, Jimmy. Will you answer my questions? That's what I need to know.'

'Yeah, I'll tell you about it.'

Miss Pimm is clearly relieved. 'Good.'

'Like I said, though, there's not much to tell.'

'Just tell me what you can. That's all I want. Will you do that?'

'Yeah. I'll do that okay.'

Dave was buoyant when they met again outside Boots at ten o'clock. Overly so. He hopped about. 'Well, that sure worked out okay,' he said.

'What did?'

'This,' Dave said, and took a small roll of notes from his pocket. 'Fifty quid for a couple of hours' work.'

'What work?'

'Just delivering something.'

'Delivering what?'

'A package,' Dave said.

'Oh, yeah?'

Dave blushed. 'Yeah. Come on. Tonight, pal, we're going to sleep in a bed. Let's go to Victoria and find a cheap B and B. Loads of them there.'

The room was small and basic, but there were two beds and they were clean. There was a wash-basin too, and Jimmy spent some time soaking his feet, peeling the socks away from the skin. His feet were red-raw, and blistered, and the hot water stung. 'Tomorrow we'll go and get you something for them,' Dave said. 'And some new socks.'

'Thanks,' Jimmy said, but his voice was surly.

'What's up with you?' Dave wanted to know.

'Nothing.'

'Come off it. It's me you're talking to. I know when something's up.'

Jimmy took his time about drying his feet, pressing the towel on to them rather than wiping. Then he climbed into his bed.

'Not speaking, huh?' Dave asked, keeping his tone bantering.

'I thought we were mates.'

'We are,' Dave said, suddenly sounding anxious.

'Then why are you lying to me?'

'About what?'

'About how you got the money.'

Dave put out the light and got into bed. For some time he lay there, saying nothing. Then he asked, 'You really want to know?'

'Yes.'

'You won't like it.'

'You went with one of those queers, didn't you?'

Dave made a grunting sound.

'Didn't you?'

'It's no big deal. Got you a bed for the night, didn't I?'

Jimmy said nothing for a while. Although he would never have admitted it, he was feeling jealous, jealous and annoyed that someone, some casual pervert, had alienated Dave from him.

'It was nothing, pal,' Dave insisted. 'Just did it to get us a few quid. All I did was lie there and let him play with it.'

'It doesn't matter,' Jimmy said finally.

'Had to do *something*,' Dave offered as defence.

'Yeah,' Jimmy said.

'*And* we've got a few quid to eat tomorrow.'

'Yeah.'

'We still mates?'

'Yeah.'

''Night then.'

''Night.'

'Nervous?' Constable Hogan asks.

'About what?'

'Court.'

'Hadn't really thought about it.'

'No need to be. They'll just ask you to plead and then set a date for the trial.'

Constable Hogan gathers up the lunch tray. 'How's everything?' he asks then.

'Couldn't be better,' Jimmy tells him.

'Saw your Mum?'

'Yeah.'

'No problems?'

'There's always problems, ain't there?'

Constable Hogan smiles. 'Like that?'

'Like that,' Jimmy says. 'I could murder a fag.'

The constable puts the tray back on the bunk, and lights a cigarette, passing it to Jimmy. 'Have to wait 'til you've finished it.'

Jimmy shrugs. 'Is it true they're questioning Dad?'

'Yes.'

'What about?'

'Just routine.'

Jimmy looks up out of the corner of his eye. 'Oh. That's okay then.'

'You're a fool, Jimmy Crichton,' Constable Hogan says sadly.

'I've known that for years.'

'You know what I mean.'

Jimmy sucks on the cigarette.

I'm not a fool, Cameron, Mum said.

You are if you give any credence to—, Dad began.

Don't treat me like a child.

If you act like a child—

Stop it! Mum snapped.
And Dad thumped out of the house, slamming the door.

And another time:
Guess what I got you today, Jimmy, Dad said.
Dunno.
Guess.
You're always buying him things, dear, Mum interrupted, and sounded irked.
He deserves to have things. Don't you, Jimmy? Here—what do you think of that!
Great, Jimmy said and looked at the digital watch.
Tells you everything, Dad said.
Great, said Jimmy again.
You spoil him, Mum said like she did every time Dad gave him something.
It's only a watch, Dad insisted.
How many boys of his age have a watch like that? Mum wanted to know.
Ah, but Jimmy's a special boy. He's *my* boy, aren't you, Jimmy?
Yes, Dad.

'Finished?' Constable Hogan asks.
   'Thanks,' Jimmy says, and stubs out the cigarette. 'Tell me something—after court tomorrow, do they take me away straight away or do I come back here first?'
   'You'll come here while they arrange transport.'
   'Will you be here?'

'Tomorrow—Tuesday. Yes, should be.'

'Can I see my dad before I go?'

'I should think so.'

'And you'd be there—at the visit, I mean?'

'I could arrange it if you want me to be there.'

'Okay.'

'You want me to? You want to see your dad?'

Jimmy nods slowly. 'Yeah. If you're there.'

'Can I ask you something now? Why do you want to see him?'

'Something I want to say.'

Constable Hogan nods now. 'Fine. Leave it to me. I'll let you know this evening before I go off duty what the situation is.'

'Thanks.'

'You know, don't you, that I'll have to report anything significant that I hear?'

'Yeah, I know that,' Jimmy says, and then adds quietly, 'That's why I want you there.'

'Right.'

'Right,' Miss Pimm says. 'Our last little chat for a while,' she adds. 'I might be talking to you again when you're on remand, but that's not certain.'

She places the packet of cigarettes and the matches on the table, and tells Jimmy, 'You know Inspector Carter. He's just sitting in.'

'Okay.' Jimmy says.

Miss Pimm busies herself for a few minutes, opening her notes and writing something down, a heading it looks like since she writes it in capitals and underlines it. 'Where would you like to start?' she asks.

'Anywhere you want.'

'Well, tell me how you first met Mr Cooper?'

Jimmy looks puzzled. 'Who?'

'Mr Cooper. The man you killed.'

'Oh, was that his name? Yes, of course it was. They told me when they charged me. I'd forgotten. Met him? A week ago, I suppose. About that anyway.'

'I take it you didn't know him well?'

Jimmy shakes his head.

'Where did you meet him?'

'Just on the street.'

'Did he speak to you or did you speak to him?'

'I spoke to him.'

'Why did you do that? I mean—do you—did you often go up to strange men on the street and talk to them?'

'I'd seen him around. I sort of knew him.'

'I see.'

'See him?' Dave asked. And when Jimmy nodded, he added, 'He's my old punter.'

'Lovely,' Jimmy said wryly.

Dave giggled. 'Well, he's sure as hell not lovely, but he's okay.'

Over the past few weeks Dave had been seeing the man on a more or less regular basis. He had been given money and gifts—clothes mostly, and he had even got some for Jimmy, useful things, underwear, socks, and a thick pullover that was a bit too big for him. But over that same period Dave had changed. He had become almost furtive, Jimmy thought, always scooting off saying he'd forgotten to do something, or forgotten to make a phone call. And when he didn't make an excuse he just vanished for a few hours without explanation. His moods had become tricky too. One minute he was in great form, laughing and joking, and the next he was sitting morosely on his bed, looking dejected, and not talking at all. He was jumpy too. Any sudden noise seemed to set him on edge. At other times he went off into kinds of dreams, not hearing a word Jimmy said, and he had taken to talking to himself both when awake and asleep. Jimmy was worried, but each time he tried to find out if something was wrong

Dave scoffed at him and told him not to be such an old nag. There was nothing wrong. He was fine.

'You want to meet him?' Dave asked.

Jimmy eyed the punter. 'Hell, no.'

'Come on,' Dave urged. Meet him. Just for a laugh. He won't eat you. Come to that he might *get* us something to eat. I'll get him to take us to the Steak House,' Dave said, and was already crossing the street towards the man. Jimmy followed, hunching his shoulders.

'Davey!' the man exclaimed. 'I didn't expect to see you at this time of day.' He swept his eyes over Jimmy. 'And who's your little friend?'

'Him? Oh, that's Jimmy. We're old mates.'

'Hello there, Jimmy,' the man said in a friendly enough way.

Jimmy nodded.

'He's *very* pretty,' the man observed.

Jimmy turned away, and felt his face redden.

'Sorry, mate,' Dave put in quickly. 'He doesn't do anything.'

'Really?' the man sounded surprised.

'Really,' Dave insisted.

'Nothing?'

'Nothing.'

'What a shame,' the man said. 'And what a waste too.'

'You've enough on your plate with me,' Dave said, making quite a joke of it, and laughing.

The man gave a small snigger. 'True. Very true. But . . . ah, well, if he doesn't, he doesn't, I suppose.'

'He doesn't,' Dave said, and now sounded a bit narked.

'Why is it the really pretty ones never—'

'Let's go, Dave,' Jimmy interrupted.

'Yeah,' Dave said. 'We've got to go.'

'Will I see *you* tonight, Davey?' the man asked.

'Yeah. Okay. Same place?'

'Why not.'

'He's creepy,' Jimmy said, once the man had gone.

'Naw. Just the way he talks. You're *very* pretty,' Dave mimicked.

'Sure I am,' Jimmy said, and they both laughed. 'Thought you were going to get him to take us for something to eat?'

145

'Shit! I forgot. Hell, *I'll* take us for something to eat. Still got enough left, and I'll be making some more tonight.'

'Can I—' Inspector Carter interrupts.

'Of course,' Miss Pimm says. 'You don't mind, do you, Jimmy?'

Jimmy shakes his head.

'Just to get things straight,' the inspector says. 'You'd seen this man—Mr Cooper—around, isn't that what you said?'

'Yes.'

'Around where?'

'Just around. Soho and places.'

'But you hadn't spoken to him before?'

'No.'

'Had you seen other boys speaking to him?'

'Yes.'

'Did you know any of those boys?'

'Didn't *know* them. Knew them to see, that's all.'

'Didn't it strike you as peculiar that this man should speak to boys?'

Jimmy shrugs. 'You see all sorts in Soho.'

'Did you know *why* he might speak to boys?'

'I guessed.'

'You knew then what was going on?'

'Sure.'

'But you hadn't been with him?'

'No.'

'Had you been with any men?'

'No.'

'You're sure?'

'Yes, I'm sure.'

'Never?'

'Never. I didn't go in for that shit.'

'Right. Thank you, Miss Pimm.'

'So, what made you go and talk to him when you did, Jimmy?' asked Miss Pimm.

146

'I was looking for someone.'

'Who?'

'Just a kid I'd met.'

'And why were you looking for him?'

'He sometimes had hash.'

'And you thought this man, Mr Cooper, might know where he was?'

'Just thought he might.'

'Had you seen the boy with Mr Cooper?'

'A couple of times.'

'Do you know the boy's name?'

Jimmy shook his head. 'No.'

'And did Mr Cooper know where he was?'

'No.'

'And that was the first time you'd spoken to Mr Cooper?'

'Yes.'

'Right,' Miss Pimm says a bit breathlessly, not having dared to breathe too deeply during her interrogation lest she lose the thread.

'Tell you one thing. We're going to have us the best damn Christmas we've ever had,' Dave said, throwing a handful of money into the air and letting the notes float down onto Jimmy's bed.

Things had certainly taken a turn for the better, financially anyway. Four nights a week Dave catered for his punters, and with the money he earned they had managed to find a small bedsit in Brixton. It was just the one room with a kitchenette curtained off in one corner. It had two narrow beds, a wooden table with one leg a bit shorter than the others, three rickety kitchen chairs, one armchair (an ancient affair from which the horse-hair stuffing oozed) and a moulting carpet. The bathroom on the landing was shared with three other bedsits. But the boys had done the bedsit up after a fashion. They now had a second-hand portable TV, and a ghetto-blaster, and, as a joke, Dave had bought Jimmy a teddybear—something for my wee mate to cuddle, he had said, giggling enormously.

'There's a hundred quid there, and more on the way,' Dave announced. 'Got two punters to pay me tonight and only serviced one,' he added, hopping about and scratching his arm.

'What's up with your arm?' Jimmy asked.

'Huh?'

'Got fleas or something?'

'Oh. Ha. No. Just itchy.'

'Maybe got a rash.'

'Maybe.'

'Give us a look,' Jimmy said.

'Naw. It's okay. It's nothing. Will you listen to what I'm telling you? It was crazy. I went with old Greg—the guy you met—and there was this other queer there too. All he did was sit and watch. Never moved at all. Never even took his hat off.' Dave burst out laughing. 'Jeez. Just sat there and watched through these really thick specs. Anyway, when Greg and me were done this guy just stood up and said goodnight, and left. So, Greg and me got dressed and had a drink, and then *I* left.' Dave sat down on one of the kitchen chairs, but almost immediately he was up again, pacing around.

'Will you sit down?'

'Huh?'

'Sit,' Jimmy said. 'You're driving me cracked.'

'Oh. Yeah. Right,' Dave said, but he didn't sit down. 'And when I got outside the house the other guy was waiting for me. You want to hear what he did?'

'Can't wait.'

'He just handed me forty quid, and said, thank you, and raised his hat—raised his fucking hat—and walked off. Christ, Jimmy, a few more like that and we'd be laughing.'

From the beginning Dave had always told Jimmy about his escapades. It was as though by sharing them, and laughing about them, he made them harmless and funny, made them into some sort of hilarious joke, obliterating all sadness from them. He liked to embellish them too, Jimmy knew, nearly always exaggerating the possessions the punters had, making it sound as if those possessions were, in a way, his. 'Anyway, we've got a hundred quid in the kitty now so

tomorrow—know what we're going to do? I'll tell you, pal. We'll go
out together and get us a tree and loads and loads of decorations.'

'Dave—'

'And a turkey. You want a turkey? We'll get a turkey.' Dave was
jumping about the room, gesticulating. 'What about a pudding? Got
to have the old pudding, don't we?'

'Dave—I won't be here.'

'What d'you mean—you won't be here. Of course you'll be here.
Where d'you think you're going to be?'

'I've been thinking—'

'Ah-ha. I knew you'd been up to no good,' Dave said.

Jimmy didn't laugh. 'I feel like a right shit letting you do all that
stuff and me just living off you. I—'

'Bullshit,' Dave snorted. 'You're not living off me. I'm just helping
you along. Can you get money off the buroo? No. Can you get a job?
No. So—'

'I hate you doing—'

'It's only a laugh,' Dave told him. 'Look, when we've got enough
cash together we'll pack it all up and go back to Glasgow. Okay?'

'No, it's not okay.'

'Come on, Jimmy. We're doing nice now. I like sharing with you.
Makes me feel—well, important if you must know.'

'It's not that—it's those—'

'Don't worry. They're okay. They're old blokes who wouldn't hurt
a fly.'

'Yeah, that's what they said about that shit who picked up young
boys and chopped them up.'

Dave ignored that. 'Can we just have a good Christmas together and
then we'll see. Please?' he pleaded. He hung his head and faked
crying, making monstrous sobbing noises. 'I don't want to be alone,'
he wailed.

Jimmy started to laugh.

Dave beamed. 'Good. That's settled. Come on, up off your arse.
Let's go see about a tree.'

'And this meeting took place, you say, about a week ago?' Inspector Carter interrupts, apologising to Miss Pimm with his eyebrows.

'About that,' Jimmy admits.

'And where were you living at the time?'

Jimmy frowns. 'What d'you mean?'

'Just what I said—where were you living?'

'Nowhere. Anywhere,' Jimmy lies.

'That can't have been very pleasant,' Miss Pimm puts in. 'Did you not—even at that stage—think about going home?'

Jimmy shakes his head.

Dad loved Christmas. He chided Mum for trying to be blasé about it. He insisted that the three of them decorate the tree together, and they all took turns in stirring the pudding mixture.

Really, Cameron, you're worse than a child, Mum said.

You've got to get into the spirit of things, Dad insisted.

The whole thing has got out of hand, Mum said. It's totally commercial now.

Only if you let it, Dad said. I've noticed *you* like getting your presents as much as anyone, doesn't she, Jimmy?

I'm just as happy with something small and inexpensive, Mum argued. Okay, Dad told her. I'll remember that. Leave me all the more to spend on Jimmy. Right Jimmy?

There you are, Dad said, standing back, and looking at the tree. Switch on the lights, Jimmy. That's your job.

Jimmy switched on the lights, and they all laughed when nothing happened.

Must be a loose one, Dad said, and started to trace the lights, screwing in the tiny bulbs tighter. And suddenly the lights came on. *Now* it's Christmas, Dad said.

It's very pretty, dear, Mum said. Even nicer than last year, she added, but that meant nothing since she said the same thing every year.

Like it, Jimmy? Dad asked.

Jimmy nodded.

And then, day by day, parcels were put under the tree, and Dad really enjoyed doing that too. He liked to trick everyone, putting small gifts in huge boxes, and joking, There's no point in trying to guess what *that* is, Jimmy.

Don't tease him, Mum said.

It's part of the fun, Dad said.

He won't sleep a wink, Mum said. Not that he's sleeping well anyway.

Don't see much for me under the tree, Dad said, pretending to be heartbroken. Don't I get anything?

Dave was proud as Punch of the little tree. He sat on the floor in front of it, his legs pulled up beneath him. His eyes shone as he gazed at the little lantern-shaped lights that flicked on and off. 'Brilliant,' he said mostly to himself. 'Like it?' he asked Jimmy.

'Brilliant,' Jimmy said too. He sat down beside Dave.

'Yeah,' Dave agreed.

And together they sat there, staring at the tree, saying nothing more, just staring.

Dave didn't go out that evening. They stayed in the bedsit and were strangely quiet as if too much talking would break some spell they had created.

Someone knocks on the door of the interview room. 'Come,' says Inspector Carter, and Constable Hogan sticks his head round the door.

'Sorry, sir,' he says to the inspector. 'Can I have a word with Miss Pimm?'

'Excuse me,' says Miss Pimm and leaves the room.

In a couple of moments she looks back into the room and says, 'Inspector—?' and the inspector goes out.

Jimmy keeps his eyes fixed on the door, wondering what has happened. He suddenly feels cold, and shivers. He goes to light a cigarette, but his hands are shaking so he doesn't bother. He is relieved to see that Miss Pimm has a slight smile on her face when she and the inspector come back. He cocks his head.

'I understand you've asked to see your father after you've been to court,' she says.

Jimmy nods.

'Well, that's been arranged.'

'Thanks,' Jimmy says, and finds he has stopped shaking.

'And your mother has sent you in some clean clothes.'

'Thanks.'

'I notice you didn't ask to see your mother too,' Miss Pimm points out, cocking her head to give the statement significance.

Jimmy says nothing.

'Was there any particular reason for that?'

'No point,' Jimmy says.

'Surely—'

Jimmy looks away and ends the speculation.

'And how are we going to cook it?' Jimmy asked, gaping in amazement at the enormous frozen turkey Dave had brought home and dumped proudly on the table.

'Huh?'

'It'll never fit in the oven.'

'Shit! I never thought of that.'

And then they were laughing, rolling about the place, trying to speak but failing. 'Maybe—maybe we could cut it in half and cook it in two lots,' Dave suggested, meaning to be serious. But that seemed hilarious also, and set them off again. 'Oh, Jesus,' Dave moaned, holding his side, then flopping onto his bed and smothering his laughter with the pillow.

And perhaps it was this unexpected and rare enough moment of pleasure that made Dave suggest later, 'Hey, what about if we have a party?'

'A party?'

'Yeah. Why not? We'll find ourselves a couple of lassies and have a few drinks and a few laughs.'

'Okay,' Jimmy agreed, although he didn't seem that enthusiastic.

'Only if you want,' Dave said.

'Yeah. Sure. Why not?'

'Okay. Let's make ourselves pretty and go and see what we can find.'

'That'll take hours.'

'What will?'

'You, making yourself pretty.'

'Up yours too,' Dave said, and leapt off the bed. 'I'm what they call ruggedly handsome.'

'Oh yeah?'

'Yeah. In the Clint Eastwood, Steve McQueen mould I am.'

'Boris bloody Karloff.'

That spurred Dave into giving a ludicrous imitation of Frankenstein, waddling with stilted strides about the room.

'Where we going to go?'

'The Poppy. No bother,' Dave told him. 'You'll see. They'll be falling over us. We're irresistible.'

And maybe he was right since from the moment they arrived in Piccadilly and settled themselves on the steps under Eros, quite a few of the girls sitting there showed interest, a coy interest it was true, but an interest nonetheless. And Dave glowed in the attention, preening himself, but trying to be very nonchalant about the whole thing. 'So,' he said to Jimmy. 'What's your fancy?'

Jimmy was beginning to feel pretty mortified by the experience. He had never been with a girl. True, he was excited by the prospect, but scared also, terrified of being humiliated. Would he do it right? Would he, indeed, get it up? Would it be big enough? 'Dunno,' he said.

'What about those two? They look okay,' Dave said. 'The two there eating the chips.'

Jimmy looked. The two girls spotted him looking, and giggled, and began whispering to themselves, pretending, of course, not to have noticed. They were pretty enough, both about fifteen, maybe sixteen, both blonde although one had her hair closely cropped. 'They're okay,' Jimmy said, trying not to sound overenthusiastic.

'I'll go get them then,' Dave said with some bravado, heaving himself to his feet and sauntering over to the girls. In no time he was back, bringing the girls with him. 'Got news for you, pal,' he said, grinning. 'Morag here is from Dundee too.'

'Oh?' Jimmy looked up.

'That's Morag,' Dave said, pushing the girl with the long hair forward a bit. 'This's Jimmy.'

'Hi Jimmy,' Morag said.

'Hello,' said Jimmy. 'What part of Dundee?'

'Albert Street.'

'Oh,' said Jimmy again. The name meant nothing to him.

'And you?'

'Broughty Ferry.'

'Posh.'

'Very.'

'Okay you two,' Dave interrupted. 'You can get to know each other when we get back to the house. Let's go.'

As Jimmy stood up Morag turned to Dave and asked, 'You ever see that film on the telly—*Leaving?*'

'No. Why?'

Morag shrugged. 'You look like one of the laddies in it, that's all.'

Dave looked really pleased.

'Doesn't he, Pauline?' Morag asked her friend.

'Does a bit. The ugly one you mean.'

'Yeah,' agreed Morag, and they both giggled.

'Let's go if we're going,' Dave said.

'Clint Eastwood, eh?' Jimmy whispered to Dave as they waited to cross over to the tube station.

'Yeah, well, what would these two know?'

They sat on the floor with their backs to the beds and watched *Top of the Pops*. Dave had bought some lager and they drank it from the cans, sharing the cans, Dave with Pauline, Jimmy with Morag. They didn't say much, just sang along with the songs they knew, and once Dave said, 'He's really crap,' when Michael Jackson's latest video was played, and Pauline agreed, 'Yeah. Really crap.' And when Wet Wet Wet appeared Morag sighed and said, 'He's lovely.'

'He's crap too,' Dave said.

'No he's not,' Morag insisted.

'You only say that 'cause he's from Scotland.'

'He's lovely,' Morag insisted again.

When the programme was over Dave got up and turned down the volume, leaving the picture to flicker away in silence. He rolled a couple of joints and passed one to Jimmy. Then he sat down again, putting his arm around Pauline's shoulder. Jimmy put his arm around Morag's shoulder. And later when Dave started to kiss Pauline, Jimmy started to kiss Morag. And later still, when Dave and Pauline stripped and got into Dave's bed, Jimmy asked quietly, 'You want to?'

'Yeah. All right,' Morag said.

As soon as they got into bed Jimmy found himself shaking uncontrollably. He had no idea why, and was furious with himself. There was no sign of an erection, and the grunting and sighing from Dave's bed didn't help. He pawed Morag in a tentative way. He kissed. He gave little sighs of his own. He squeezed her breasts like he'd seen actors do in films, and was pleased when she gave a few tiny gasps. He wondered if he could feign drunkenness, pretend to fall asleep. Indeed, he was on the point of trying that when Morag bent over him and started running her tongue down his chest. She lingered by his belly button, kissing it, and suddenly the shaking stopped. He felt a slow, indescribable glow sweep over him, and a throbbing in his loins. Then she had his penis in her mouth, sucking ravenously, up and down, and he felt himself swell and swell. He put his hand on her head forcing her down. Morag groaned. Jimmy groaned.

'Oh, Jesus. Oh, Jesus,' Dave's voice said, straining.

Jimmy waited a minute, and then said, 'Oh, Jesus.'

And then Morag was moving upwards again, kissing his body, her lips like feathers blowing across his skin. She found his mouth and kissed him hard, forcing her tongue into his mouth, making a small whispering noise. Then she kissed his ear, whispering, 'Oh, Jimmy. Oh, Jimmy.'

Oh, Jimmy, Dad said from somewhere.

Jimmy froze.

'What's wrong?' Morag asked.

'Nothing,' Jimmy said, but he felt his penis slacken, felt it flop.

Morag's hand reached down and felt the slack organ. 'There *is* something,' she whispered.

'It's nothing,' Jimmy said, kissing her on the lips to stop her talking since Dave and Pauline had finished and were very quiet. 'Just the drink,' he added.

'Oh,' said Morag, and rolled back on the bed.

'We can do it in the morning.'

Morag said nothing.

But they didn't do it in the morning. Dave woke Jimmy, shaking him and saying, 'Are you staying there all day?'

Jimmy sat up with a start. 'Where—' He looked about him.

'Oh, them? They've gone. Didn't want them hanging round our necks all day, did we?'

'No.'

'Gave them a few quid and sent them packing.'

'Oh.'

'Good, though, wasn't it?'

'Yeah. Great.'

Dave grinned. 'You sure as hell made enough noise about it.'

'*I* did? What about you? Grunting like a stuck pig.'

Dave laughed. 'Part of the act, pal. Part of the act.'

Jimmy lay back in his bed and pulled the blankets up to his chin. But Dave was having none of that. He reached out and stripped the blankets off, and started to tickle Jimmy. They rolled about on the bed, Jimmy screaming as Dave held him down. Then, exhausted, they lay still. Suddenly Jimmy felt Dave's penis throb against him. He felt his own penis start to stir. He looked into Dave's eyes. 'Better get up,' he said.

Dave stared at him for a moment. 'Yeah,' he said, 'Guess we better.' He rolled off the bed, turning his back to Jimmy. He took his boxer shorts from the floor and slipped them on. Then he stretched. 'Jesus, I'm starving.'

'Me too.'

'Well, get your arse up and we'll go and get a burger.'

'Right.'

They sat in McDonalds eating their burgers and drinking coffee. For the first time since they had met there seemed to be nothing to say. Dave even seemed to be avoiding Jimmy's eyes. Then, suddenly, he said, 'Fuck this. We're mates, aren't we?'

'Sure we are.'

'So we'll forget it.'

'Forget what?'

Dave grinned. 'Yeah. Exactly. Forget what.'

And as if by magic they were back on an even keel, chatting away, laughing at nothing. Indeed, it was if they were even closer than before. And perhaps it was because of this that Jimmy felt hurt when Dave said, 'Well, I better make a move.'

'Oh?'

'Yeah.'

'Oh.'

'You be okay for a few hours?'

'Sure.'

'I left a few quid on the telly. You can take that if you need it.'

'Thanks.'

'Right. Well, I better shift. See you later.'

'Okay. Take care.'

'I will.'

Jimmy watched Dave leave McDonalds. He watched him pass the window with his swinging, cocky stride. He felt suddenly very lonely. But then Dave stuck a thumb in the air and winked at him, and everything was all right again. He winked back, and waved and felt that his wave meant something to Dave since he straightened his shoulders, and bounced off, giving the impression he hadn't a care in the world.

Alone in the bedsit Jimmy stared about him. Then, deliberately, he moved across to Dave's bed and lay down on it, cuddling the pillow. He closed his eyes.

—Oh, Jimmy, Jimmy, Morag said.

—Oh, Jimmy, Jimmy, Dad said.

Suddenly Jimmy was crying although he had no idea why. He sat up. Then he swung his feet off the bed, and threw the pillow away from him. Roughly he wiped his eyes with his fists and walked across to the television. He took the money Dave had left and shoved it into his pocket. He stared at the Christmas tree.

—Don't see much under the tree for me, Dad said, pretending to be heartbroken. Don't I get anything?

For one horrible moment Jimmy wanted to rip the tree to shreds. He wanted to pull the decorations off one by one and stamp on them. He wanted nothing to do with Christmas. Then he shook his head, and left the bedsit.

XI

Jimmy bought Dave a cheap watch from Ratners, one of the ones you didn't have to wind. He bought some fancy Christmas wrapping-paper too, and parcelled the watch up carefully. He stuck a little tag to one corner, and wrote, TO DAVE, MY PAL, on it, printing the words. And he had spent a long time choosing a Christmas card. It was a pretty card, showing two small children, two boys, in Victorian dress gazing in amazement at a festooned tree with hundreds of gaily wrapped presents underneath it. A fire glowed in the background, and holly had been placed behind the paintings that hung on the walls. A furry dog lounged in front of the fire looking comfortable and warm and well fed and loved. Jimmy thought about putting the names Dave and Jimmy over the two children on the card, but didn't. Inside he wrote, FROM JIMMY, and left it at that.

When he had finished wrapping the present and writing the card he felt really pleased with himself. It was, it dawned on him, the first time he had ever *wanted* to give someone a gift. He didn't *have* to give Dave anything; he certainly wouldn't expect anything. Not like at home when you had to get something for everyone whether you wanted to or not. Mum even gave presents to people she didn't like.
—I really don't know why I bother getting them something. It's not as if we *liked* them.
—Well, why do it then? Dad asked.

—Oh. It's Christmas, Mum said vaguely. Anyway, they'll give us something. They always do.

—Only because you send them one.

—Well, I'm not going to be the first not to, and have them talk about us.'

—So keep on sending them something, Dad said, sounding exasperated.

Jimmy was about to put the watch under the tree when it struck him that Dave would never wait until Christmas morning before opening it. He decided to hide it. The only safe place, he thought, was up on the top shelf in the kitchen. It was a ridiculously high shelf, reachable only by standing on a chair. He carried one of the chairs into the kitchen and stood on it. He put the present and the card on the shelf, and pushed them towards the back. He was about to get down when he noticed the long, narrow metal box. He felt a sudden tingle of excitement. Maybe someone, the last tenant, had left treasure behind them. Maybe it was stuffed with twenty-pound notes. Maybe doubloons. He grinned to himself. He took the box from the shelf and jumped off the chair. He sat down, and anxiously prised open the box.

It took quite a while for the significance of this find to register. He stared unblinkingly at the syringe for a long time. He thought he could see blood on the needle, Dave's blood, but he could have been mistaken. Slowly he closed the box, and returned it to its hiding place. Then he carried the chair, the present and the card back to the main room. He put the present and the card on the table, and sat down, fixing his eyes on them. For the best part of an hour he sat there, feeling miserable. Then he got up and shook himself. He put the present under the tree, and the card on Dave's pillow. Then he lay down on his own bed, closed his eyes, and curled himself up into a tight little ball.

He was still lying like that when Dave came home.

'For me?' Dave asked, opening the card, his eyes bright. He sat on his bed while he read it. 'You know something, pal? That's the first Christmas card I've *ever* had.'

Jimmy smiled. 'Dave—'

'The very first,' Dave went on. 'Here,' he added suddenly, 'give us a cuddle.' And then he was sitting beside Jimmy, holding him in his arms, and saying, 'Thanks, pal, thanks, pal,' over and over.

'Dave—' Jimmy tried again.

'You're the best pal anyone could have,' Dave was saying, and then—'What?'

'Nothing. Just—'

'Just what, pal?'

'Just—oh, shit. Just that there's a present for you too.'

Jimmy sat back. His eyes were watery, but they were shining now too.

'A pressie? Where?'

'Under the tree.'

'Wow,' Dave said, and made a dash for the tree.

'Hey, you can't open it now,' Jimmy told him.

'Why not?'

'Not 'til Christmas morning.'

'Aw, go on. Let's open it now.'

'No.'

'Get me right in the Christmas mood, it will.'

'No. You'll just have to wait.'

'I can't.' Dave had taken to hopping about again.

'You'll have to.'

'Please?'

'No.'

'Ever so fucking pretty please?'

'No.'

'You're a wicked, hard man, Jimmy Crichton.'

'It's not lucky.'

'What you mean—not lucky.'

'It brings nothing but bad luck if you open your pressie before Christmas.'

'Really?'

'Really.'

'Okay. Okay then. Don't want any bad luck now, do we?'
'No,' Jimmy said. 'No,' he said again, sadly.

Because it's unlucky, Mum explained, going on to say something about the Three Wise Men but getting lost in her story, and saying, It's just unlucky, again.
Oh, let him open one, Dad said.
Definitely not, Mum said.
One won't hurt, Dad tried.
Not even one.
Sorry, Jimmy, Dad said. Did my best.
Don't pander to him, Cameron, please.
Dad made a face.
And don't make faces either, Mum said.
All this for one little present, Dad said.
It's the principle, Mum insisted.
Hear that, Jimmy? Dad asked. It's the principle. Your mum's a great one for her principles. You have to wait until Christmas morning, I'm afraid, Dad told Jimmy. But don't you worry. You and me, we'll get up really early on Christmas morning and we'll come down here together without telling your mother.
That's very nice, Mum said coldly.
Oh, Alice, for heaven's sake, I'm just trying to make Christmas a happy time for the boy.
And leaving me out, Mum said.
It was just—just—Dad began.
I know what it was, Mum told Dad.
   But, anyway, on Christmas morning Dad woke Jimmy very early, long before Mum was awake, and they sneaked down to the tree. And for every present that Jimmy opened Dad kissed him, and cuddled him, and fiddled with himself. And Jimmy hated opening his presents.

'Means, of course, I've got to get you something now,' Dave said with mock annoyance.

'No you don't,' Jimmy told him.

''Course I do. Was going to anyway. Anything special you want?'

Jimmy shook his head.

'Leaving it to me, eh?'

'That's right. Use your imagination.'

'You might be sorry you said that,' Dave said, and laughed.

'Doubt it.'

'Hey, come on. Let's go out and celebrate. Celebrate my first ever Christmas card. My treat.'

'It's always your treat.'

'I know. I *like* it that way.'

'*I* don't.'

'Your turn will come, pal. Don't you worry. Your turn will come.'

'So the first time you actually spoke to Mr Cooper was six days before Christmas?' Miss Pimm asks, getting herself back on track after the interruption.

'Yes. About six days. Maybe seven.'

'But you had seen him before?'

'Yes.'

'Many times?'

'Yes.'

'Talking to boys?'

'Yes.'

'Had you spoken to any of those boys about him—about Mr Cooper?'

'No.'

'But you knew what was going on?'

'I guessed.'

'And you're quite sure that Mr Cooper never approached you before the night you killed him?'

163

'I told you. No. I mean, yes, I'm sure.'

'So, you spoke to him one night, and you killed him the next, is that right?'

Jimmy nods. 'Yes.'

'Something must have happened then?'

Jimmy says nothing.

'Jimmy? Did you hear me? Something must have happened to make you kill him?'

Jimmy keeps his head down.

'You said you'd tell me,' Miss Pimm says.

'I will. In a minute,' Jimmy says.

So Miss Pimm waits, and Inspector Carter waits, and Jimmy leaves them waiting.

'Jeez, I'm stuffed,' Dave said.

'Me too,' Jimmy agreed.

They had gone to Piccadilly and gorged themselves on pizza slices from a little shop on the corner of Shaftesbury Avenue.

'Good, though,' Dave said.

'Terrific.'

'What you want to do now?'

Jimmy shrugged. 'Dunno.'

'Fancy a lager?'

'Yeah, I fancy one. Where?'

'The pub I use is just up the road.'

'They won't serve me.'

'Yeah they will. You look about eighteen anyway. And if you're with me, it'll be okay.'

'This the place you meet—?'

'Yep,' Dave said quickly, and started walking.

'Isn't there somewhere else?'

'Sure, but if we're in luck we won't have to pay here,' Dave said, and kept walking. 'Anyway, it's a tourist attraction. You know that guy you were talking about—the one who picked up boys and chopped them to bits and stuffed them down the drain? Well, this is one of the places he operated from. Come on. It'll be a laugh.'

'Ha ha,' Jimmy said.

'See? You're enjoying yourself already.'

'Very funny.'

'Jimmy, you really do need to tell us,' Miss Pimm says.

'I'm thinking,' Jimmy tells her.

'We don't have a great deal of time,' Miss Pimm says, but not in a cross way.

'No, it's all right, Miss Pimm,' Inspector Carter says. 'Let him have the time he wants.'

'Very well,' Miss Pimm says.

Jimmy lowers his head again, and pretends to think.

The pub was on Dean Street. It was quite full when Dave and Jimmy went in. 'You stay here by the machine,' Dave said. 'I'll get the drinks.'

Jimmy stayed by the fruit-machine, and stared about him. Some of the men at the bar, most of them elderly, eyed him but pretended not to. There were some stools against the wall under the windows, and on these some boys were seated. They watched Jimmy too, but with only vague interest. One of them got up and went to Dave, spoke to him and returned to his stool. He and his companions got into a huddle, speaking rapidly. Jimmy looked away, wishing Dave would hurry back. But he didn't seem to be in any hurry. He was chatting away to a man at the bar. Not earnestly, but in a bantering sort of way. Then the man nodded, and paid for Dave's drinks.

'Told you,' Dave said, bringing Jimmy his lager. 'Told you we wouldn't have to pay.'

Jimmy sipped his drink.

'That's the one I was telling you about. The one who only likes to watch—remember?'

'Yeah, I remember. Looks a right pervert.'

Dave laughed.

'Something really creepy about those eyes.'

'It's just those thick specs he wears. He's okay.'

'Let's go somewhere else,' Jimmy said.

'Jesus, give me time to finish this first, will you?'

'They're all gaping at me.'

'Sure they are. You're new blood. They always gape at new blood. I've told them you're not available, so don't worry.'

'Gives me the willies.'

'It's just a laugh,' Dave said.

Jimmy finished his lager quickly. 'Look, you stay. I'll just buzz home.'

'But we're out together.'

'I'm in the way.'

'No you're not.'

'I know I am. Bet he wants to get off with you,' Jimmy said, nodding at the man in the thick spectacles.

'Well, as a matter of fact—'

'See. Told you. I'll be okay. You stay and I'll go on home.'

'You sure?'

'Yeah. I'll be fine. Just don't like the place.'

'Okay. See you later.'

'Yeah.'

'And tomorrow I'll get you a present like you've never had.'

Dave didn't come home that night. It was late the next morning when he got back. He staggered into the bedsit, and collapsed on to his bed without a word. Almost immediately he was crying to himself.

'Jesus, Dave, what's happened? What's the matter?'

Dave said nothing, just sobbed away to himself.

Jimmy sat on the bed beside him, and put a hand on his back, shaking him a little. 'Hey, come on, pal. Tell me. What's the matter?'

'Bastards,' Dave said.

'Who is?' Jimmy asked. 'What the hell happened?'

'Just leave me, will you?'

'Hey, it's me. Jimmy.'

'Just leave me.'

'Look, get your clothes off and get into bed,' Jimmy said. He took off Dave's shoes and socks. 'Turn over, will you, so I can open your belt?'

'Just leave me.'

'No I won't.' Jimmy fumbled until he got the belt open, and started to pull Dave's jeans off. When he got them down over his buttocks he stopped.

'Christ, Dave, you're covered in blood.'

'Just fuck off, Jimmy and let me alone,' Dave shouted. He reached behind him with one hand and covered himself with his jeans again.

'Dave—' Jimmy said.

'Just fuck off!' Dave screamed.

Jimmy sat on the bed the whole afternoon, wanting to touch Dave, wanting to comfort him, wanting to tell him that everything would be okay.

'He was a bastard,' Jimmy says suddenly, making Miss Pimm jump a bit and look shocked, making Inspector Carter blink and lean forward, putting his elbows on the table. But neither of them says anything for the moment. 'He was a real bastard,' Jimmy says, and looks away as he feels tears filling his eyes.

'Take your time, Jimmy,' Inspector Carter says.

Jimmy takes the handkerchief Miss Pimm had given him from his pocket and blows his nose noisily. He swallows, and blows again.

'We know something about Mr Cooper already,' Inspector Carter says, 'so we can guess what might have gone on.'

Jimmy shakes his head.

'Did he try to have sex with you?' the inspector asks.

Jimmy shakes his head, and sniffles.

'Did he try anything with you?'

'Not with me.'

The inspector and Miss Pimm exchange puzzled glances. Miss Pimm looks as if she's about to speak but the inspector stops her with a small frown. 'He did something to someone else?'

Jimmy nods.

'A friend of yours?'

'My best friend.'

The inspector leans back. His face looks very sad to begin with, and then becomes angry. 'Do you know what he did to this friend of yours, Jimmy?' he asks quietly.

'Yes.'

'Will you tell us?'

Eventually Dave fell into a fretful sleep, tossing a lot, and muttering wildly to himself. It was after six, and dark, before he woke up.

'All right?' Jimmy asked.

'Yeah,' Dave said.

'Want some tea?'

'Got a fag?'

Jimmy lit a cigarette and passed it to Dave. Then he went into the kitchenette and put the kettle on the small gas ring.

'I'm sorry, pal,' Dave called.

'For what?'

'For shouting at you.'

'Never heard a thing,' Jimmy told him.

Dave swung his legs off the bed, wincing. He felt his buttocks, and then stared at his fingers. 'Christ!' he swore.

'You're covered in blood,' Jimmy said. 'I nearly got a doctor.'

'It's okay,' Dave said. 'No need for a quack.'

'What happened, Dave?'

'Raped me, didn't they,' Dave said. 'I've got to get cleaned up,' he added, and headed for the bathroom on the landing.

'Want any—' Jimmy began, but Dave was already shaking his head.

'Raped him, didn't they,' Jimmy tells Inspector Carter, and sees Miss Pimm recoil a bit with shock.

'Cooper raped your friend?' the inspector asked, sounding incredulous.

'No. He just watched. Got some other shits to do it,' Jimmy says. 'Something to do with some film.'

Now the inspector nods understandingly, and turning to Miss Pimm, he says, 'That fits.'

'Did your friend tell you exactly what happened, Jimmy?' Miss Pimm asks in a tone that suggests she's a bit scared of hearing what happened.

Jimmy nods. 'Yeah, he told me,' Jimmy says bitterly.

'I know it's painful and difficult for you, but would you tell us?' Miss Pimm asks.

Jimmy closes his eyes tightly, and keeps them closed all of the time while he tells them.

Dave came back into the room after cleaning himself up. Even though he had washed and combed his hair he still looked haggard. And he had lost his cockiness. There was a terrible haunted look to his eyes, and his hands kept twitching.

'Here, drink this,' Jimmy said, passing him a mug of hot tea.

'Thanks, pal,' Dave said, taking the tea and lowering himself gingerly on to his bed, propping his pillow behind him. For a long time he just stared at his tea, giving small, convulsive gulps, and blinking a lot. Then, finally, he said, 'I'll kill that bastard.'

Jimmy said nothing, but he nodded.

'Just sat there watching, with this grin on his face,' Dave said.

'Who?' Jimmy asked.

Dave gave a little start. 'Huh?' he asked.

'Who sat there grinning?' Jimmy asked.

'That Harold bastard. The little shit with the glasses. I showed him to you the other night.'

'Oh, yeah,' Jimmy said. 'I remember.'

'Said it was just a little film he wanted to make. Promised me two hundred quid for it.'

Almost as an afterthought Dave reached for his jacket and began to search in the pockets. Slowly he pulled out a large wad of notes. He stared at them, then let them slip through his fingers and scatter on the floor. He gave a wry laugh. 'Got back to his place and started having a few drinks. Didn't think anything of it,' Dave went on, almost as if he was talking to himself. 'There was me, and him, and about four other blokes. Anyway, after a bit he said something like, "Let's make movies," and we all went into the bedroom. One of the others started playing with me, and then the next thing I knew they were holding me down and this big bastard was on top of me . . .' Dave stopped talking, and started to shudder.

Jimmy went to the bed and put his arm about Dave's shoulder. 'It's okay, pal,' he whispered.

'He just sat there saying, "That's right, my lovely Turk, give it to him",' Dave said, turning away as he started to cry. He looked up at the ceiling, blinking to stop the tears, and added, 'Christ, Jimmy, I was screaming my head off with the pain.'

Jimmy rubbed his back. 'I know, mate.'

Dave shook his head. 'Oh no you don't. Not pain like this.'

(Dad put his hand over his mouth and forced himself inside.)

'I know, Dave,' Jimmy said again.

But Dave still shook his head. 'And he kept on and on at it. And they were laughing and jeering and the shit with the camera was saying he wanted another angle and—' Dave was getting hysterical, and Jimmy said, 'Shush, pal.'

—Shush, Jimmy, said Dad.

'Shush, Dave.'

Miss Pimm has gone quite white.

'I'll organise some tea, I think,' Inspector Carter says, looking a bit pale himself. He goes to the door and says something to a policeman outside. Then he comes back to the table and sits down again. He clears his throat. 'That's all your friend told you, Jimmy?' he asks kindly.

Jimmy nods.

'And I take it Cooper was the man who just sat and watched?'

'Yes.'

'You don't know who the others were?'

'No.'

'Your friend didn't mention any names?'

Jimmy shakes his head. 'Just what I told you.'

A policeman knocks on the door and brings in a tray with three cups of tea on it. He is young, fresh-faced, and clearly nervous at serving the inspector. The cups rattle on their saucers. The inspector passes one cup to Miss Pimm, who says, 'Thank you,' politely, and another to Jimmy, who nods, and says, 'Thanks.' After he has tasted his own tea, and grimaced slightly, the inspector says, 'I'll need to know the name of your friend.'

'Dave,' Jimmy tells him.

'Last name?'

'Dunno,' Jimmy lies. 'Never knew it. We never gave last names.'

'Is he from Scotland too?'

'Yes.'

'What part—of Scotland? Dundee?'

'Perth,' Jimmy lies, and doesn't know why.

'Where can we find him now?'

'Dunno,' Jimmy says, adding, 'Honest I don't,' as the inspector gives him a dubious, disbelieving glare.

'No idea?'

'None. Haven't seen him since he told me what happened to him.'

The inspector, for reasons of his own still looks sceptical. 'Just vanished into thin air?'

'Vanished anyway,' Jimmy says.

Dave was in a bad state. He was jittery, and kept moving about the room, unable to settle. He kept going to the curtain by the kitchen and peering in. Then he'd look at Jimmy, and move away again. 'Go on,' Jimmy told him.

'Go on what?' Dave asked.

'I found it this morning.'

For a moment Dave froze. 'Found what?'

'Your tin.'

Now Dave tried to brush the whole thing off. He gave a hoarse laugh. 'Oh, *that*. Yeah, well—you know—' He waited for Jimmy to say something, but when Jimmy stayed silent he added, 'It's just—hell, you know.'

Still Jimmy said nothing. He couldn't think of anything to say. He lay back on the bed.

'Yeah—well since you know—' Dave said, and gave another awkward, forced laugh. 'Since you know I may as well—'

'Kill yourself,' Jimmy heard himself say.

'It's not like *that*, pal,' Dave told him. 'Really it's not. I only take a bit now and again to keep me going.'

'Sure.'

'I'm not an addict or anything.'

'Course you're not.'

'I'm not. Really.'

'Okay. I believe you.'

'It just gives me a buzz.'

And a buzz was what he needed now, it seemed. He took a chair with him as he went into the kitchenette.

'Look, pal, I just want to get out by myself for a while—okay?' Dave asked. He was quite calm now, moving easily as he put the chair back in its place. No twitching. 'I just want to do a bit of thinking.'

'You're not going to—' Jimmy began, worried, and sitting up. Dave gave him a wide friendly smile. 'I'm just going to take a wander and think a bit. That's all. Don't worry.'

'You're coming back?'

'Course I'm coming back. Think I'm going to miss opening my pressie?'

'Okay then.'

'See you in a bit.'

Jimmy went to the bedsit window and watched Dave walk up the street. He seemed to be limping now, but he wasn't weaving or anything. And maybe he sensed Jimmy looking at him since he turned round, looked up, and waved.

Jimmy never saw him again.

XII

For two days and late into the evening of both days Jimmy hunted for
Dave. He hung about outside the pub in Soho, hoping for a sight of
him, but he never turned up. He wandered all over Soho, down every
little street, asking other boys if they'd seen him—some hadn't even
heard of him, some thought they knew him but couldn't be sure, and
the few who did know him hadn't seen him. Once, on the second
evening, Jimmy thought he saw Harold Cooper crossing the street,
and raced after him. But when he caught up with the man it wasn't
Cooper, nothing like him except that he was small and wizened and
wore rimless spectacles. 'Sorry, mate,' Jimmy said.

'That's all right,' the man said. 'Are you—'

Jimmy raced away again. For an hour he stood outside the pizza
place near Piccadilly. He sat under the statue of Eros, his eyes
searching the faces that sat there, and the ones that crossed the roads.
And each evening when he got home he would lie sleeplessly on his
bed, hoping to hear the sound of Dave coming up the stairs, staying
awake on purpose since he felt it would be unkind to be comfortably
asleep if Dave came back.

'So, when your friend told you what had happened to him—was that when you decided to kill Cooper?' the inspector asks.

Jimmy smiles to himself at the way the inspector has stopped calling the man 'Mr' Cooper, and screws up his face, thinking. 'No. I mean, I suppose I *wanted* to kill him then—well, no, not *kill* him, just beat the shit out of him,' he admits.

The inspector nods. 'That came later?'

Jimmy raises his eyebrows quizzically.

'Your decision to kill him.'

Jimmy nods. 'A couple of days later. After I couldn't find Dave,' he says. Then he shakes his head. 'Crazy really. If we hadn't got the turkey I probably would never have killed him.'

'I'm sorry?' says the inspector, and, 'What was that?' says Miss Pimm, both of them speaking together.

'We had this huge frozen turkey, see? For Christmas. Dave got it. I don't know where. We had it in the—' Suddenly Jimmy stops, and looks quickly away. In his mind's eye he sees the turkey lying in the sink, but if he says that they'll want to know where the sink was. 'In the—?' he hears the inspector ask.

'In this bucket. Yeah, one of those metal buckets that someone had thrown out 'cause there was a bit of a hole in it. Anyway, we had the turkey in the bucket, and we hid the bucket under the steps that went down to the basement of a derelict place. We put a dustbin lid on top of it. And a concrete block on top of that.'

'And this derelict building was where?' Miss Pimm asks.

'Oh, it's out—out Shepherd's Bush way.'

'Could you show us where it is?' the inspector asks.

Jimmy shakes his head. 'No way. No idea how to get to it. I mean, I know roughly but—'

'It doesn't matter,' the inspector tells him. 'You were saying that in some way the turkey made you kill—'

'Oh, yeah. Well, we'd nicked this knife from some hardware shop— big long thing, it was, and sharp as a razor. We were going to use it to carve the turkey—that's if we ever got it cooked.' Jimmy hears himself giggle at that. He doesn't want to laugh. It just comes out. 'We left the knife in the bucket with the turkey. So, anyway, when I couldn't find Dave I went back, just to see if the turkey had thawed a bit—'

'So, you were able to find the place then?' the Inspector said.

175

'Just lucky. Got off at the right station. Can't tell you which one though.'

'You said Shepherd's Bush.'

'Yeah—*out* that way. Not Shepherd's Bush itself, though.'

'Go on.'

'So, I remember taking up the knife and prodding the turkey,' Jimmy says, adding, in a dreamy sort of way, 'Really funny, you know. Just sticking the knife into that bird made me feel—I don't know. Sort of powerful. And with Dave not being there I thought about sticking it into the bastard who'd, well, who'd made him leave, I suppose.'

Jimmy stared at the turkey in the sink. It had almost thawed, but not quite. It was a grey-pinky colour. He took the carving knife from the drawer beneath the sink, and started to prod the turkey. It made a funny sucking noise each time he stabbed it. He changed his grip on the knife. Then he held it over his head and brought it down on the carcass with all the force he could muster. Again and again he did this. He knew he was being crazy. He wanted to stop, but he couldn't bring himself to stop. And when he did, breathless, the turkey was in shreds.

Jimmy stared down at the lacerated bird for several moments. Then he ran the blade of the knife under the tap, and wiped it dry. He took an old magazine from under the sink and wrapped the knife in it, putting it carefully on one side. Then he put on his anorak, and combed his hair. That done he slipped the wrapped knife up under his arm, under the anorak, and for a few minutes practised walking with it there. Satisfied, he looked about the room, memorising it: the two unmade beds, his Christmas card to Dave still poking out from under the pillow; the money Dave had let fall on the floor; the Christmas tree, unlit and looking drab for that, Dave's watch, wrapped, beneath it. Someone was in for a surprise when they found the money and the watch, he thought. Then, but shit, I'm coming back, aren't I? Satisfied, he put out the lights, locked the door behind him, and padded off down the stairs.

Inspector Carter finishes his tea and puts his cup on the tray. He pushes the tray to one side. 'So it was while you were—while you were stabbing the turkey that you decided to do the same to Cooper, is that right?'

'I guess so,' Jimmy admits. 'Although it wasn't really like that. I mean, I don't really know *what* I meant to do.'

'Did you go out looking for Cooper?' Miss Pimm asks, but making her question sound more like a suggestion.

'Oh, yes. I wanted to find that bastard all right. I think I had some idea of just threatening him. Maybe giving him the odd stab or two. Just to frighten him.'

'And you found him?'

'Yes,' Jimmy says with a firm nod.

'Where?'

'Soho, of course. I didn't *know* he'd be there. I mean I hadn't seen him when I was looking for Dave. But it was the weekend, Friday, so I sort of guessed he'd be hanging around.'

It was strange. For a while all his eyes would focus on were the rimless spectacles. It seemed almost as if that was all there was: a pair of glasses peering at him.

For over an hour Jimmy hung about in the vicinity of the pub in Dean Street, staying as long as he dared near the door, and then criss-crossing the street, even wandering up as far as Frith Street before coming back to loiter near the pub again. He was on the point of moving off again, had, indeed, made up his mind to go into the amusement arcade across the way from where he could still keep an eye on the pub entrance, and had looked to his right for traffic when Harold Cooper loomed into his vision. For a moment they both stood stock still, Jimmy suddenly apprehensive, while Cooper had a quizzical look on his thin face. 'Haven't I seen you before, young man?' he asked.

'How would I know?' Jimmy said.

Cooper laughed. 'Indeed, how could you. Stupid of me.' He continued to eye Jimmy. 'Going for a drink?'

'Can't,' Jimmy told him. 'Not old enough.'

'Or no money?'

'Both.'

'You can come in with me.'

'Naw. I'm not into drinking anyway.'

Cooper gave a thin smile. 'And what are you into?'

Jimmy shrugged. 'This and that,' he said, and felt the knife suddenly grow heavy under his arm.

'I *see*.' Cooper used his middle finger to flick an invisible irritant from the tip of his nose. 'You like videos?'

'Depends.'

'Good videos,' Cooper said, and then bending forward slightly, '*Very* good videos.'

Jimmy put on his most innocent face. 'Sure, yeah, I like good videos.'

'I've got quite a collection.'

'That's nice.'

'You must come and see them sometime.'

'Yeah, thanks, well, I won't be here—here in London, that is— much longer.'

'Oh?'

'Got to get back home. My mum's sick, so—' Jimmy let that hang.

'Oh, dear, I am sorry. When are you—?'

'Tomorrow if I can,' Jimmy said quickly.

Harold Cooper thought about this, keeping his eyes fastened on Jimmy. 'Well,' he said finally, 'if you're not doing anything *now* . . . And perhaps I could help you a little towards your fare.'

Jimmy warned himself not to appear too anxious. Dave had told him about that once. 'The trick,' Dave maintained, 'is not to appear too anxious. The harder to get you play the more interested they become, and the more interested they become the more they want you, and the more they want you the more they pay,' he had explained in one breath, gasping ludicrously at the end of it. 'I dunno,' Jimmy said now doubtfully, shaking his head.

'You need only stay an hour or two. Just long enough to see a video,' Cooper told him, sounding reasonable.

'You live far?'

'Not too far.'

'Got a car?'

'Yes, I've got a car.'

'Drive me back, will you?'

'If I don't I'll see you have enough money for a taxi.'

Still Jimmy hesitated.

'You'll enjoy yourself,' Cooper assured him.

'Where's the car?'

'Just up there. In the square. Two minutes' walk.'

'And you'll see I get back okay?'

'I promise.'

'All right then.'

'Good,' Cooper said, beaming a wide smile.

Together they cut through on to Frith Street and made their way up to Soho Square. Cooper kept trying to make conversation, but Jimmy only gave terse or grunted replies. He was now feeling scared. He was scared of Cooper. He was scared of what he might be about to do to Cooper. He thought about turning tail and scampering off as fast as he could. 'Here we are,' Cooper told him, stopping by a grey Granada, and fumbling for the keys.

'Nice,' Jimmy told him.

'It goes.'

'Bet it does.'

Cooper held the door open for Jimmy, and closed it behind him when he got in. Then he walked round the car to get into the driver's seat. Jimmy watched him through the windscreen. And as he watched he eased the knife from its wrapping. He got it out from under his anorak and laid it on the seat beside him, keeping his hand on it; as Cooper got into the car he tightened his grip on it. Cooper put his keys in the ignition. Before starting the engine he turned to Jimmy and said, 'Off we go then.'

'A couple of points, Jimmy,' Inspector Carter says. 'Did you approach Cooper or did he approach you?'

Jimmy frowns, trying to remember. 'Neither really. I turned round and there he was, staring at me.'

'But it was Cooper who made the first—how can I put it?—the first advance? It was him who suggested you go back to his place to watch videos, was it? I mean, did you lead him on? That's what I mean.'

Jimmy frowns again. 'I wanted to lead him on, but I didn't have to.' He gives a tired smile. 'Even tried playing hard to get, I did.'

'And he kept insisting?'

'Not insisting. Just making it sound like as if I'd have a good time, and that he'd give me money.'

'Did he say how much money?'

'Said he'd give me enough for a taxi back if he didn't drive me. Oh, and, yeah, he said he'd help me with my fare back home.'

'I don't follow that,' Miss Pimm says.

'I'd told him I was coming home the next day.'

'Oh,' says Miss Pimm, but in a way that hinted she still didn't really understand.

'So you walked with him to his car,' the inspector says.

'Yes.'

'Did he do anything to you in the car?'

'No,' Jimmy says. Then he gives another tired smile. 'Didn't have time to, did he?'

'You just killed him?'

Jimmy nods. 'Sounds funny when you say it like that—"you just killed him".'

Jimmy felt something snap within him. It was so real he thought he could hear a small crack like a twig breaking. He saw Cooper's face grinning at him. He saw Dave's face in anguish with tears rolling down his cheeks. He saw Dad's face looking blankly at Mum as he denied everything. He saw his own face, terrible and haunted, glaring insultingly at him. He pulled up the knife and plunged it into Cooper's side with all the strength in his body.

For what seemed a very long time Cooper did nothing. He just kept staring at Jimmy with a puzzled look on his face. Jimmy stabbed him again. Cooper half turned, grappling for the door. Jimmy stabbed him between the shoulders. Then the car door was open and Cooper was out, staggering across the square, screaming for all he was worth. Jimmy froze, watching as Cooper toppled over. He lay on his back, his legs kicking, his arms waving wildly. Jimmy leapt out of the car and ran towards him, hearing Cooper's screams get louder and louder as he got nearer. He knew there were people about him. He could hear them shouting at him. He knelt down beside Cooper and kept stabbing him, screaming at him, until he gave a curious gurgle and lay still. Then, everything went black.

Miss Pimm has already started tidying up her papers, and the inspector has gone to the door. He is talking to someone in the hallway.

Miss Pimm gives a great big sigh. 'Well, Jimmy, that's it for the time being.'

'Yeah, I guess it is.'

'I *will* see you before they take you to the remand centre. Just one or two things. All right?'

'Fine.'

Miss Pimm stands up as a police sergeant comes in and says he's ready to take Jimmy back to the cell. 'I won't say goodbye, then,' she says.

'No,' says Jimmy. 'It's *au revoir*, isn't it?'

Miss Pimm looks very sad. 'Yes. Yes, Jimmy, it is.' She tucks her papers under her arm and walks across the room.

'Miss Pimm,' Jimmy calls.

'Yes, Jimmy?'

'You know I'm seeing my dad tomorrow?'

'Yes.'

'And you know that Constable Hogan is going to be there?'

'Yes, I had heard you asked specially for him to be present.'

'Yeah, well, make sure you have a word with him after the visit, will you?'

'Why is that, Jimmy?'

'Just have a word with him.'

Miss Pimm nods as if she understands. 'I'll do that. Thank you, Jimmy.'

'You're welcome. You have a nice day now.'

Miss Pimm smiles. 'Thank you.'

XIII

'Ready then?' Constable Hogan asks.

'Ready as I'll ever be,' Jimmy tells him. 'Worse than going to court, this is,' he adds with a smile.

'You don't have—'

'I know.'

'How was it anyway?'

'Court? Nothing to it. Wasn't there all that long. Just had to plead.'

'For what it's worth,' Constable Hogan says as they make their way from the cell block, 'For what it's worth the feeling is it won't go all that hard on you.'

'Like what—fifty years instead of life?' Jimmy says and laughs. 'Jeez, you're sure you going to stay with me here?'

Constable Hogan says, 'Sure. There'll be two of us.'

'Two, eh? Become dangerous overnight, have I?'

Constable Hogan chuckles.

'Two heads better than one?' Jimmy suggests.

'Something like that.'

'Oh, I get it.'

Jimmy has never seen Dad so dishevelled. His hair is all mussed up, and if he has shaved he's missed bits out here and there. The bags under his eyes are dark brown, and the eyes themselves are bloodshot. He is sitting at the table with his head in his hands when Jimmy is brought in.

'Hi, Dad,' Jimmy says tentatively.

Dad looks up, eyes Jimmy for a moment, and then stares at the two policemen standing by the door. Then he looks back at Jimmy, and nods. 'Jimmy,' he says. 'You look well.'

'I'm fine. The clothes Mum sent in help.'

'The clothes maketh the man,' Dad says vaguely.

'Don't, Dad. The clothes *don't* maketh the man.'

Dad gives a wan smile. 'You're right. My mistake. A Freudian slip,' he says.

'Yeah,' says Jimmy. 'Were you in court?' he asks, more for something to say than anything else.

Dad shakes his head.

'Oh.'

'What happened?'

'Nothing much. Just asked me how I wanted to plead, and I said "Guilty", and that was about that.'

It's Dad's turn to say, 'Oh.'

'Dad—' Jimmy begins, but the look Dad gives him makes him stop. It is a pleading look, but there is something frantic about it. 'You all right, Dad?'

Dad nods. 'It's just—just we've nothing to say to each other, have we?'

'I thought we might have.'

'No,' Dad insists. 'No, we *don't*.'

Suddenly Jimmy feels angry. It is as though all the anger he has kept pent up inside him has burst. 'Jesus, Dad, you really are something else.'

Dad looks away.

'Here's me, about to be banged up and have the key thrown away and all you can come up with is that we've nothing to say.'

'What *can* we say, Jimmy?' Dad asks with something approaching a sly, sneaky look towards the policemen.

184

'You could always try saying you're just a bit sorry,' Jimmy tells him.

Dad's manner changes just as suddenly as Jimmy had felt his anger rise. He bangs his fist on the table. *'Me* say I'm sorry? *Me?'* he shouts. *'You're* the one who has caused all the trouble. You and your lies. Take a good look at me, Jimmy. Look at me, damn you. Look what you've done to me.'

And Jimmy looks. He looks in amazement, his eyes wide, his mouth slightly open, an incredulous smile on his lips. 'Okay,' he says quietly. 'I've looked. Now you look at me, Dad. Look at what you've done to *me.'*

But Dad doesn't look. He gets quickly to his feet, sending his chair crashing away behind him, making the policeman with Constable Hogan take a tentative step forward but stopping when Hogan gives a tiny shake of his head. Dad walks about the room for a few minutes. Then he rounds on Jimmy, leaning his hands on the table and bending over. 'You know what you are, Jimmy Crichton? You're evil. That's what you are. Evil,' Dad says between his teeth with a hissing sound.

Furious, Jimmy shouts, 'Must have got it from you then.'

'That's right. Keep at it. Blame me for things I never did. Try and drag me and your mother down with you.'

Jimmy is crying now, crying with anger and pain. It isn't going at all like he wanted it to. All he had wanted was for Dad to take him in his arms and say, say something like, 'I'm so sorry, Jimmy,'—say it quietly to him, without anyone else hearing, just a secret apology between them. Instead Dad is saying, '—only—evil—kill,' is what Jimmy hears. He leans back in his chair, balancing it on its back legs. The tears have stopped. A terrible coldness has entered his eyes as he watches his father, his hands squeezed into tight little fists, making his knuckles go white as Dad says, 'How any son of mine could kill a . . .'

Now Jimmy jumps to his feet, leaning on the table too, pushing his face close to his father's. 'That was the easy part,' he says in a fierce whisper. 'All I did was pretend it was you.' His voice starts to rise. 'Every time I stuck that knife into the bastard I told myself it was you.' He is shouting now. 'And every time he screamed I told myself it was you screaming the way you made me scream only I didn't put my hand over your mouth to shut you up!' Jimmy hears his own voice screaming now. 'I wanted everyone to *hear* you scream so they'd know what I was doing!' He feels himself start to shake. He hears himself give a tiny laugh. 'You know something? That bastard wasn't half the bastard you are.' He steadies himself, consciously controlling the shakes, and stands erect. 'And you know something else? I don't even hate you. All I do is pity you, Dad. You're—you're—oh, fuck it,' he says, and turns away, walking over to the door. 'Let's get out of here,' he says.

Constable Hogan holds the door open. For a second Jimmy hesitates. He looks back, hoping Dad will say something. But Dad hasn't moved. He looks frozen, still standing over the table, leaning forward. Jimmy shakes his head, and walks out.

'Well,' Constable Hogan says, 'it's time to go.'
Jimmy stands up.
'How d'you feel?'
'Like shit.'
Constable Hogan nods.
'How is *he*?'
'Oh, he'll be all right. Got to think of yourself now, lad.'
'Yeah.'
'Got everything?'
'Oh, yeah. I've got everything.'
Jimmy leaves the cell and walks slowly up the corridor. At first he seems to drag himself along, his shoulders hunched. But then he straightens himself up, and by the time he reaches the van that is to take him to the remand centre there is a spring in his step. 'You know what?' he says to Constable Hogan. 'I kind of think you were right.'
The constable winks at him. 'There you go.'
Jimmy likes that. He gives a huge smile. 'That's right,' he says. 'Here I go.'